AAH THE STORY OF S
A Love Story

By Eleanor Sinclair

Copyright c2019

Snazzycat Publishing

Snazzycat Publishing, 304 S. Jones Blvd., #1642
Las Vegas, Nevada 89107

AAH, THE STORY OF S, A Love Story is a work of fiction. The names, characters, places and incidents are products of the writer's imagination or have been used fictitiously and are not construed as real. Any resemblance to persons living or dead, actual events, locales, companies and/or organizations is entirely coincidental.

Copyright 2019 by Snazzycat Publishing

All rights reserved. Except as permitted under the U.S. Copyright Act of 1976, no part of this publication may be reproduced, distributed, or transmitted in any form without the written permission of the publisher, except in the case of brief quotations embodied in critical articles and reviews.

Published in the United States by Snazzycat Publishing

Library of Congress cataloging-in-publication data

Eleanor Sinclair – author

AAH, THE STORY OF S/Eleanor Sinclair

ISBN paperback: 978-1-7347761-1-9

TABLE OF CONTENTS

Preface	5
Chapter 1 - Monday Night, August 4 East Hampton	6
Chapter 2 - Tuesday, July 29, Manhattan	26
Chapter 3 - Monday, August 4 Riverhead Correctional Facility	46
Chapter 4 - Wednesday, July 30, Manhattan	61
Chapter 5 - Monday, August 4 Riverhead Correctional Facility	74
Chapter 6 - Thursday, July 31, Manhattan	89
Chapter 7 - Thursday, July 31, Manhattan	106
Chapter 8 - Friday, August 1, Manhattan	111
Chapter 9 - Saturday, August 2 East Hampton	128
Chapter 10 - Saturday, August 2 East Hampton	142
Chapter 11 - Tuesday, August 5 Riverhead Correctional Facility	149

Chapter 12 -	Saturday Evening, August 2 East Hampton	154
Chapter 13 -	Tuesday, August 5 Riverhead Correctional Facility	199
Chapter 14 -	Monday, August 4, East Hampton	217
Chapter 15 -	Wednesday, August 6, East Hampton	281
Chapter 16 -	Wednesday, August 6, East Hampton	301
Chapter 17 -	Wednesday, August 6, East Hampton	321
Postscript -	Autumn	337
Post-postscript -	Autumn, East Hampton	351

Preface

The first draft of this book was begun in the 1990's, long before "Fifty Shades of Grey" was ever written. It is from the perspective of Michael, a twenty-five year old aspiring actor. Most of the time we don't know whether to believe him, or if he is just trying to protect himself. We don't know what is the truth and what is not.

It is a love story between Michael and Sybil, a forty something woman movie producer. Our justice system is irretrievably broken, when the one with the most money wins, both in criminal and in civil cases. There is no such thing as "blind justice." This story illustrates that.

This novel takes place in the 1990's during a sizzling hot summer in Manhattan and East Hampton. This story has more twists and turns than Lombard Street.

It is not suitable for those under the age of 18.

CHAPTER 1 - Monday Night, August 4
East Hampton

I remember the night we drove up that long winding road to a sprawling grey shingled mansion that stretched on across the well kept lawns. We got out of the taxicab at the home of a movie mogul in East Hampton. We were so happy then before we entered the party. Then much later after most of the guests left, the nightmare began. It is still so clear to me what happened that night and it haunts my every waking moment and all my nightmares.

It was the blond boy Eric. He had just turned twenty and missed his birthday party. He didn't even call to let us know he wasn't coming. Now look what he got himself into. He couldn't move but he watched us, me and Melody, as we were shoved into the room. Eric's wrists and ankles were chained to the wall. Around his neck was an iron collar. He was naked and facing the wall. An older man, Alan's friend, was beating him with the leather whip. The tall blond woman stood and watched. Eric looked scared.

"Michael, this is Eric. I think you've met before," Alan said in the most casual of manners, which made it even more bizarre. Melody, just seventeen, was in a zombie-like state, standing right next to me.

"This is what you chose Michael. You came to me. You want me to do something for you, to help you, don't you. Well, let me tell you, first it's your turn to do something for me, and your pretty little friend too."

"Alan, I think you're making a big mistake."

Alan was screaming like a madman right in my face. I could smell his boozy breath. "You do g-ddam nothing and you expect the world to roll over for you. I think you're going to roll over for me tonight, Michael, like you've never rolled over before."

He tried to grab me, but I pushed him away, and then with no warning, he punched me right in the face. I lost my balance. The older man was upon me, as he and Alan grabbed my arms and pinned them back behind me. They pushed me over to the wall next to Eric. I kicked at them as I struggled to get loose, but the two men were too strong to overcome together. Each man firmly held an arm as they chained me to the wall.

"Melody run, get out of here." She ran to the door and twisted the handle, but it was locked.

"Bang on the door. Someone will hear you."

She pounded on the door, screaming, "Someone, someone please, let us out of here. Please, let me out." She was hysterical.

The flashbacks of that horrible night keep coming back to me. It seems like a lifetime has passed, but it was actually only three nights ago. Now I find myself sitting in a jail cell in East Hampton facing Murder One for a brutal sex slaying. I saw it happen, but I swear I didn't do it. I'm being framed for it. I'm sitting here like some kind of decoy duck waiting to be hauled in front of a judge first thing in the morning. The cops say they got a confession out of me last night me after they arrested me. Lies, all lies.

How the hell did I get myself into this mess? It all began when I came to New York to find fame and fortune, and then I met Sybil.

I first met her at the Red Zone, a bizarre wacked out club downtown on the Westside Highway. It was Monday, July 28th and the city was sweltering hot, even at eleven o'clock at night. We were all standing outside on the sidewalk behind a velvet rope, waiting to be let in by the bouncer, a bulldog faced guy with a shaven head and one small gold earring.

The night club was in an old meatpacking warehouse lit up with neon outside across its crumbling brick walls. It was like a huge flashing sign welcoming all those who dared to enter. The air was so suffocating outside, you almost couldn't breathe. They say all the asphalt holds the heat, and lets it out even worse late at night. I didn't know cities could smell as bad as uncleaned pig pens.

When I was finally let in, I saw all these guys in weird

leather outfits and punk hairdos, girls with shaven heads and just a few regular looking people. I didn't know it was especially wacked out on Monday nights. The music was blasting so loud even the floors were shaking. "Y.M.C.A." was playing,, which was quite a coincidence since that was where I was staying.

Standing at the bar, I chugged down a few beers, trying to forget my troubles. The guy next to me seemed real friendly and started a conversation. He put his hand on my shoulder and asked, "Where you from? Just visiting?"

"No, I'm trying to stay here, trying to become an actor, but my money's about to run out, so this might be my last night in town."

"Hey, cheer up, who knows, maybe you'll meet someone here tonight. My budget's kind of tight right now, but sometimes talent agents and movie producers hang out here, but they only go to the top floor, a kind of private club."

"Hey, thanks, then that's where I'm heading." I drained the last of my Rolling Rock, and bounded up four long sets of metal stairs. I somehow convinced the bouncer to let me onto the top floor. It had all this weird décor, like out of Aliens. Then I saw her standing there at the back bar talking to some people.

She was sleek, with dark hair pulled back in a tight little chignon, so chic, just like in the fashion magazines, nice jewelry, not that costume stuff. I could tell it was real. She had a perfect face, and was wearing a purple silk pant suit.

She was rich and she was staring at my crotch in my tight jeans. I took a swig out of the bottle of Rolling Rock, the cheapest beer at the bar, and looked back at her. She was still looking at me while she talked to her friends. Then she was nodding, beckoning for me to come over.

Well, what did I have to lose? I looked real hard and intense at her. I could see myself slipping between her satin sheets. I hadn't been to bed with a girl for a whole week, since I left my uncle's farm in Missouri. Hell, I was outright horny and the young ladies in New York wouldn't even give me the time of day with my dusty Dingo boots. I couldn't afford to take them out anyway.

I drained my bottle, taking my sweet time, didn't want to seem too anxious, trying to play hard to get. I slowly put the bottle down on the bar and sauntered over.

"Hey cowboy, what's your name?" she asked sweetly, looking me up and down.

"Michael, what's yours?" I managed to force the words out. I didn't realize I was so nervous.

She was probably in her forties, early forties, I thought. No wrinkles. immaculately put together, nice shape, good curves.

"What are you drinking?" she asked.

"Heineken."

"Bartender. Two Heinekens."

She continued talking to her friends, a tall elegant woman and a middle aged man, as she handed me two Heinekens and nodded a toast to me. They seemed out of place for the sort of sleazy place The Red Zone was. Disco music was blasting out over giant loud speakers. There were two men in their twenties, muscular, but definitely gay, dancing on the bar in G-strings. They had real short blond hair. In the middle of them was a very tall guy in drag, a transvestite in a big brunette wig cascading down over his shoulders. A five o'clock shadow was showing all over his face just like Bruce Willis.

The drag queen was wearing red satin high heels, a short red sequined dress with fringe at the bottom, a black bra stuffed with tissue paper that was peeking out of the low cut top. They were all grinding away to the music, "Baby, don't hurt me, don't hurt me, don't hurt me no more, what is love?" The guy in drag was blowing kisses to the audience. The men at the bar were whistling and making catcalls, just like construction workers watching a pretty girl walk by. Then the drag queen started lip synching the words to the song, "Baby, don't hurt me, don't hurt me no more." The thick makeup, the extra long lashes piled high with mascara would do Tammy Baker proud. Never saw anything like that back in Missouri, but I guess this was the big city and anything goes. Out there a guy was a guy, and a girl was a babe who you made out with in the back of a pick up truck, the sun blazing as it set over miles and miles of golden fields stretching out forever in the distance, the sky turning purple and your passion rising. It seemed like a million miles away and a million years ago. I could never go back to that nothingness. I snapped myself back and stared as hard as I could into the woman's brown eyes and at her ruby red lips.

"What's your name?" I managed to ask as the words stumbled out of my mouth.

"Sybil," she said and then continued talking to her friends about producing a film that was set to start shooting tomorrow right here in Manhattan. It was starring some well known actress who used to be a singer. This could be the lucky break I was looking for. And she was hot for me too. I could tell by the way she kept looking at me, even though she was still talking to the man. As a matter of fact, it was making me want her even more, and not a minute too soon. With just $5 left in my pocket and the last night paid for at the "Y," I guess I'd be out panhandling on the mean streets of New York in the morning or something else.

Just as I was throwing back the second Heineken, she asked again, "What's your name?"

"Michael." I thought I'd already told her.

"Well Michael, wanna go?"

"Sure." She took my arm in hers and we walked down the long flight of metal stairs.

Then we were outside in the sweltering heat. A long black limo was waiting just down from the door, and as I hoped, she walked us straight over to it. The driver rolled down the window.

"Take us to the apartment, Cecil."

Cecil was a woman with short blond hair, young, pretty, wearing a chauffeur's cap and a navy-colored jacket with the monogram "S" in gold thread embroidered on both lapels. Sybil and Michael squeezed together in a corner of the dark cavernous back seat, silently sailing through the now beautiful streets of New York. Her lips were pressed hard against his. He felt he was being sucked in, she was kissing him so forcefully. The window between their compartment and the driver was half open. Soft rock was now playing on the car stereo. "Runaway train, never going back. Like a madman laughing at the rain." Michael was getting rock hard. He didn't know what she expected. He was a little overwhelmed and out of his league.

He didn't have long to find out. Her hand went down to unzip his jeans. She told him to take them off. Michael was embarrassed, but he did what she told him. Off came the boots and jeans. No underwear. Still drying in the room at the Y. She unbuttoned his shirt and he slipped that off too. Now he was sitting there stark naked and he motioned her to close the window to the driver, but she just laughed and told him to sniff some white powder. It was cocaine. She pushed him gently back and sucked at his nipples, then her tongue slid down to his navel. He knew the driver was watching through the mirror. Then Sybil pulled Michael on top of her, and before he could help it, he was exploding and exploding again and again. She pushed him off her and gave the driver an address, 14 East Fourth Street, just like that.

"This is just what the doctor ordered" she told the driver, as Sybil fixed her makeup in the mother of pearl compact. She reached for the car phone and punched in a number.

"I'm sending someone up to see you. To cheer you up.... yes right now. Guaranteed. Ciao."

She put down the phone. "I want you to do a little favor for me tonight. I have a difficult friend. She's got to be on the set early tomorrow morning for her first scenes. I'm going to drop you off at her apartment. Her much younger boyfriend just walked out on her yesterday. Go cheer her up, but be sure to get her to the set by 7:30 in the morning. I think she'll like you. We're starting production on a feature film in the morning."

I couldn't believe it, she was passing me out like a piece of meat, just flesh, no feelings, no emotions. I knew I'd already fallen for her. I never knew anyone like that back home in Missouri, so forceful, so sure of herself. I only had silly little corn-fed girls willing to do anything for me, and I mean anything.

"Sybil, I like you a lot, but I'm not a prostitute. I'm just a small town boy down on my luck. You can't pass me around like that."

"Do it as a personal favor for me, prove your loyalty to me. Make her happy and I'll see you on the set in the morning. And I promise, it'll only be the two of us together tomorrow night. We'll talk about your future," she said, as she looked at his run down Dingos as he put them back on over his well-worn socks.

He had his pride, he thought, as the limo pulled to an abrupt stop in front of a tall building.

"Go up to Apartment 18A. She's expecting you."

She didn't even tell Michael the woman's name, as she pushed him out of the door.

"Don't keep her up too late," she called out, as he stood there on the sidewalk. She was already on the car phone as he saw her window rolling up. Then the limo started pulling away from the curb. He was still zipping up his jeans when he saw a big tall black uniformed doorman smiling at him as he held the door open, inviting him to enter the ornate lobby.

My head was spinning. It was just all happening too fast.

I was in a whirlwind, I couldn't think. What the hell was I doing? Was it a set-up? I was getting very paranoid. Who was she really sending me to see? And what were they really going to do? I had no idea.

It was already 2 A.M. on the big clock as I glanced around the high ceiling lobby. The doorman was on the house phone after I told him 18A.

"There's a young man here to see you, a Mr. Michael," he smiled as he gave me a look I didn't like.

There were intricate mosaics on the immense walls, colorful scenes of a silk factory, silk worms, looms, and rolls of different colored silk material. The lobby had marble floors and tall thick columns.

"This is called The Silk Building," the doorman interrupted my reveries, as he pushed the elevator button. "Used to be a silk factory, before it was converted into lofts, duplexes and triplexes. Have a good time," he smiled as the elevator doors opened.

The doors seemed to slam shut, or was it just my nerves. Who the hell was I being sent to see? This town's too much for me. I was thinking of hitching back home tomorrow, but to what? What the hell was I doing here anyways, as I watched the floors go up one by one. The door opened onto the 18th floor and I couldn't believe my eyes, but padding down the carpeted hallway toward me, barefoot in a silk Kimono, partly opened to show off her long legs, was the tall, beautiful, more beautiful than her videos or album covers, the very famous singer Annize.

He knew she liked younger guys, but this was crazy, someone she didn't even know. She put her fingers to her lips, and took me by the hand as she led me to a red door.

Her apartment was spectacular. It wasn't New York any more, it was Santa Fe, New Mexico. It was all done to look like the inside of an adobe Indian pueblo. Even the walls were textured. There were real cactuses everywhere. She didn't say a word, but as soon as she shut the door, she leaned up against me and kissed me softly on my mouth. She then took my hand and led me down the hallway to her bedroom. It was straight out of The Arabian Nights. The bed had a purple silk canopy with gold tassels.

She unbuttoned his shirt and had him slide his jeans down to the floor. He kicked off his boots. He couldn't believe he was standing there totally naked with another woman, so soon after the first. "Here I am baby, take me by the hand, here I am baby, come and take me," was throbbing over the radio.

Annize slid off her robe. She stood there smiling at him. She was tall, bronzed, and naked like an Indian goddess, her long black straight hair cascading down over her shoulders and halfway down her back. She pressed her breasts against his well toned chest. Michael climbed in under the purple silk covers. She slid in under the bottom of the covers and pressed her body against him. Annize, music goddess, he was totally aroused by her. He noticed the little wrinkles at the corners of her eyes and mouth, that hinted of her forty-five years, but that didn't matter. He ran his hands down her body, over her small breasts.

Then he mounted her like a buck on his doe from behind, and if he was dreaming he didn't want to wake up. He rammed her gently over and over again. This time, his second of the same evening, he was able to take it longer, much longer. He rammed her slower with each thrust, over and over again, until she started moaning with pleasure. He was going to draw it out as long as he possibly could. Eventually she came with a loud cry, and he let it all explode like a bright starburst on a cloudless night.

&&&&&&&&&&&&&&&&&&&&&&&

All too soon, there was the shrill sound of the alarm clock ringing. Then the telephone chimed in. It was dawn. She was still in bed, wound around him, one arm over his shoulder, the other across his chest. It was 6 A.M.

"Shit," Annize screamed as she answered her wake up call. "Fuck Sybil, I'm not going to the set today. Let them start without me. They can just do someone else's scenes first," she said as she snuggled up against me. "Let's stay in bed together all day...."

"Michael," I offered as I could see her struggling to try to think of my name. I don't think I ever got the chance to tell her last night. As a matter of fact, I don't remember one word passing between us. Sybil said to get her to the set by 7:30. How the hell was I going to do that? How the hell was I going to tell this big star what the hell to do? Damn it, I had to think fast.

"Annize, I'd love to stay in bed with you all day, but I promised Sybil I'd get you to the set by 7:00, so why don't we go over there together."

"That bitch Sybil, I almost forgot she sent you over," she screamed as she leapt out of bed naked.

She slipped on her kimono and padded into the luxurious green marbled bathroom. We took coffee together on her private terrace. She had on large black sunglasses and wouldn't even look at me.

She just stared out at the New York skyline with the sun breaking over all those incredible buildings, their towers turning golden in the gleaming sun, the Chrysler Building, the Empire State Building. It all looked incredibly heartbreakingly beautiful. Maybe this was going to be my lucky day.

CHAPTER 2 - Tuesday, July 29, Manhattan

As Annize and I stepped out of the elevator, I walked across the lobby quickly so I could hold the door open for her as she glided through, barely beating the doorman to it. He was still on duty from the night before. Outside, there was a long stretch silver limo letting some passengers out.

"Is that Keith Richards of the Rolling Stones? I asked. There he was sauntering into the building as we were leaving. He was returning at 7:00 A.M. We entered the black town car waiting for us.

"Yeah, he lives here too," Annize said as she fixed her makeup in a mirror. After a short drive, we pulled up to a large building in the heart of the village, not far from Annize's triplex. It was just off Lafayette Street, near Union Square.

As we walked in, I saw it was a huge sound stage. Sybil was talking quietly to a cameraman who was sitting behind a big movie camera on a revolving platform. She looked up and seemed pleased to see us.

"You're right on time," she said. She took Annize's hand and led her to a dressing room. A make-up man and a blond hairdresser were waiting for her.

"Annize, why don't you go over the lines for your first scene while they take care of you."

"You're always full of good suggestions," Annize said as she smiled up at Michael. You know I'm nervous about that first scene."

Just as she promised, she didn't just throw me out the door.

"Michael, you come with me." Sybil took my hand and we went back to the enormous sound stage. I guess I performed satisfactorily for her.

"You did well. Here's a chair for you. You can watch the filming and learn some things. Then I'm taking you to lunch."

Michael sat fascinated watching the filming until noon.

Church bells rang out. The church must have been very close they sounded so loud or was it just his nerves. It was difficult spending the whole morning with the two women he had just been with the night before. He felt strange about it. He wasn't used to such things from where he came from.

"Well, I can't take you to '21' dressed like that," Sybil said disapprovingly, looking at his perfect body in his worn shirt and jeans. She took Michael's arm and they walked out to her limo. The same driver was there as the night before.

"Cecil, take us to Armani's."

Soon they were driving down Madison Avenue where all the posh people shop. Women were walking little tiny poodles in rhinestone collars or maybe they were real diamonds, Michael thought.

Then he was trying on clothes just like Don Johnson wore on "Miami Vice." Michael came out of the dressing room and modeled for Sybil who was seated in a big comfortable chair.

Some she liked, others she just nodded her head no. She ended up buying three suits, collarless shirts, shoes, belts, the works. Michael looked in the mirror. He couldn't believe the transformation from dusty cowboy to sophisticated New Yorker. He had on a charcoal grey jacket and pants, a cream colored top, Armani loafers with grey patterned argyle socks.

"Michael, leave that one on. We're going straight to lunch. I'm famished."

Now I was really starting to get somewhere. I looked like I really belonged as we walked out to the limo. Both hands carried shopping bags with the name "Armani" blazoned across them.

"Cecil, take us to '21.' I think we're ready now," Sybil laughed as she looked approvingly at Michael.

The bags were put in the trunk by the ever efficient but silent Cecil. I wondered if she knew how to talk. Maybe she couldn't, a speech impediment or something. Sybil spent the entire time on her car phone talking to someone about filming, about the first "set up" for the afternoon. She didn't even look at me. It made me kind of nervous. So I just looked out at tall the buildings as we headed to "21" for lunch.

As we pulled up, it looked like some kind of private club, on a little side street with rows of ivy covered townhouses. Short metal jockeys lined the outside stairway up to the front door, each one with a different colored vest and cap, holding an iron ring in his hand. To tether your dog or horse. I guess dog since not too many people rode their horses around the streets of New York City. I got out first and started climbing up the stairs, but Sybil laughed as she stepped out of the limo.

"No, Michael, that's not the entrance, it's down here."

He felt like a total jackass, but he was too embarrassed to say anything. He just followed her in. There was a life size horse in the waiting area, a statue of a famous race horse. The maitre'd greeted her familiarly and then took them to a table in the dark club-like dining room. There were large model airplanes hanging down covering the whole ceiling.

Just as they were being seated, Annize walked in with a man he recognized Sybil had been talking to at the club the night before. And wouldn't you know it, Annize sat down right next to Michael, and pushed her thigh right next to his. He didn't know what to say. He felt a little awkward with both Annize and Sybil at the same table, the two ladies he made love to just the night before.

"Alan, I'd like you to meet a new friend of mine, Michael. Michael, this is Alan, the man we all worship because he says whether we work or not. He controls the money."

Alan gave me a strange kind of look. I wasn't sure I liked the way he was looking at me.

"Sybil, I'm glad we're having this meeting today. Frankly, I'm concerned about this film."

"It wouldn't be little ol' me you're concerned about, would

it Alan?" Annize asked nervously.

"No, not really. Sybil, seriously, you've got too many locations out in the Hamptons. And you're planning to shoot them at the absolutely worst time of year. If you run into any problems, that could add time, lots of time, and time is money. Can't we change those locations?

"No Alan, absolutely not. I feel they're essential to the film. And if we postpone past the season, we're not going to make the distribution deadline."

"Damn it, Sybil, you could save weeks if you'd shoot those scenes on a sound stage and just use a blue screen and a lot of second unit stuff."

"Alan, you know I hate blue screens. We've got to get the flavor of the actual locations."

"O.K. Sybil, have it your way. You're the producer, but don't come crying to me if you get in trouble. You know there are only so many strings I can pull for you."

"That's what I'm counting on, Alan."

"Well, don't count on too much. You know even though I adore you to death, my first obligation is to the studio."

"I know Allan. And I also know you don't let your good friends down."

"Hey, enough shop talk. Didn't we come here to eat. Garcon, menus please."

"Yes Mr. Prescott, right away Mr. Prescott. May I take your drink orders now?"

Everyone ordered cocktails except Michael. He ordered a Heineken, in a bottle.

Before he knew it, Annize's hand traveled up his thigh and was on his crotch. Good thing it was hidden by the table cloth. He tried to move her hand away without anyone noticing, but he couldn't budge it. It was there like a lead brick.

"Sybil, I'd like Michael over tonight, you know, to help me rehearse my lines for tomorrow's shoot. O.K. Sybil?"

What, she didn't even ask me. Was I already Sybil's property? Jeez.

"Sorry, no can do. Michael's busy tonight. He and I have some business to discuss."

"Sure, uh huh, some business all right." Annize shot her a funny kind of look, like who the hell was she kidding. "You're just too mean, Sybil."

"No, really, he's reading a part for me, for my next production."

"Oh, really, is Michael an actor?" asked Alan.

"Well Alan, he's an aspiring actor."

"Oh Sybil, not another protégé."

I wasn't sure I liked Alan's comment, particularly the way he said it. I was looking back and forth at them and feeling like they were arguing over a scrap of meat and I wasn't even there. Shit, I had to get out of there, but maybe, just maybe, she was serious about helping me.

"Here," Sybil leant down and took some pages out of her briefcase. She handed them to Michael. It was dialogue from a script.

"Hot off the presses, Michael read this. It's from a new erotic thriller, like "9 ½Weeks." I want you to hear this too, Alan. We're going to need twenty million for this one, just for production costs. We're thinking of Sharon Stone and a hot new unknown guy for the male lead,"

Sybil looked at me. "So go ahead, read it, like they say," she intoned as she lit her cigarette in a long silver holder, "there's no time like the present."

"Sybil, I'll listen, I'll always listen, but I'm not promising anything. Remember, they want names, names on major parts, particularly with a budget like that, twenty mil just for below the line." Alan sounded concerned.

"Never mind him, Michael, just go ahead. You're reading for me. I'm the producer."

"You mean right here, now?"

"Yeah, why not."

"O.K. I guess. I mean, there's all these people here."

Sybil laughed, "Well you better get used to that. We usually have at least one hundred crew on set."

"O.K., well here goes . . . "

"No, Michael, always read it over first. Let me know when you're ready. Never, never, ever read that cold for anyone."

The pressure was really building. Here he was doing his first reading in New York, with no prep, and all these people were looking at him, waiting for him to do something, in a damn restaurant. His face turned three shades of red. Michael thought, how the hell was I going to read that scene. The guy was doing all the talking, to a woman, like a crazy X-rated monologue, describing how he was going to touch her all over while she sat in see-through lingerie with her legs spread, thrown over the back of a chair. And to top it all, Annize still had her hand pressed on my crotch, trying to get me aroused.

"Are Messieurs and Mesdames ready to order?" The waiter startled Michael and he dropped the pages to the floor. He saw Annize's legs under the table as she shifted, showing her black mesh panties.

"Go ahead, Michael, study the script. We don't have much time. We've got to get back to the set right after lunch."

"You're just saying that 'cause I'm here today," Alan said as he looked over the menu.

"You're right Alan. Otherwise, we'd take our time," Sybil laughed. "Michael, I'll order for you, so you can look over the script."

The waiter took everyone's order and scurried away.

He didn't know how he got through it. He started reading as softly as he could, but it seemed like everyone in the restaurant was listening. He felt like it was the most embarrassing moment of his life, but he starting reading.

"Annouk, I want to see more of you. I want to see all of you. Pull down your stockings, pull them down to your ankles. Let me brush you like a feather all over your body."

Then the script said he mounted her while she sat in the chair. Michael was sweating up a storm, like a prize fighter just out of the ring. He took the linen napkin and wiped his forehead. He thought he was making a total fool of himself, but everyone at the table was totally silent. And to make matters worse, he was now rock hard from Annize rubbing her hand over his crotch. She had started while he was holding the script and there was nothing he could do about it.

Sybil was smiling now and said, "Very good, Michael, very good, not bad."

Michael made sure the large linen napkin totally covered his lap. He was totally aroused. He tried to push Annize's hand away, but she squeezed his hand so hard it hurt. He let out a little sound, "Oh" just as the waiter laid the appetizers on the table.

The waiter gave him a disapproving look, as he put the smoked salmon with capers down in front of him. Hungry and starving as he was, with one White Castle burger all day yesterday and nothing but coffee this morning, Michael wasn't sure he could eat one bite. He could barely hear Sybil speaking to him.

"Michael, your reading was very good, just a little rough around the edges. I think you could use a little polishing at the Strasberg Institute. You could be the next Marlon Brando."

"Do you mean the famous school where DeNiro and Pacino studied?" Michael asked.

"Yes. Did you know even Marilyn Monroe studied there? She was the best, no one can touch her to this day in comedy. Just look at her films, "Gentlemen Prefer Blonds,"

"And 'The Seven Year Itch . . . ,'" added Annize, trying to catch Michael's attention.

"Isn't that the one with her white dress blowing up over the subway grate as the train whooshes by? Michael was trying to sound knowledgeable.

"And don't forget she was absolutely brilliant in "Some Like it Hot" Sybil said with emphasis on the word "brilliant."

"And I screwed her," Alan interrupted.

"Alan, you crude bastard, isn't anything sacred to you?"

"No Sybil, absolutely nothing . . . except you of course." Alan took her hand and kissed it.

"Alan, somehow I don't believe you, not for one damn minute."

"Sybil, it's true. It's 'cause you're probably the only one who never bows down to anyone to get what you want in this business. As a matter of fact, I've noticed you don't even let anyone get near you, except who you want to." Alan glanced over at Michael.

"Come on Alan, you must want something with all this flattery. What is it?"

"It's for me to know and you to find out." Alan looked again at Michael. He was getting a bit tipsy, as he leant toward Michael.

"I'm going to make you the next heartthrob of America. I'm sending you to study acting at the Strasberg Insitute, the best, right here in New York," Sybil said as she lifted her fork.

"Acting classes, that's great." Michael felt a warm rush of feelings toward Sybil. No one had ever helped him before. He had worked hard on his uncle's farm since he was a kid. He thought, I just want to hold her and make passionate love to her all night, better than that first night in the limo. I couldn't believe it was only last night. It feels like a zillion years ago. I want to make love to her like a man to woman, that's what I really want. I couldn't believe it, she was going to come through for me after all, just like she promised. I wanted to pinch myself to make sure I wasn't dreaming. Not too bad, he thought. Here I am at "21" in an Armani suit, sitting here with all these glamorous people, and just yesterday I was practically starving, almost out on the street. He looked down at the big juicy steak the waiter put in front of him. It was about three inches thick and very rare.

"I think you're going to need this, Michael, to keep your energy up. Aren't you going to eat? You know the saying, 'Youth is but a fleeting thing, Carpe Diem, seize the day."

Michael could hardly eat, but he managed to gulp down a few bites. Soon everyone was finishing their dessert, the lightest fluffiest cake he had ever seen. It was almost like eating air with a thin golden crust on it.

"They call it a SOO-FLAY," Annize told him as he looked curiously at it.

"Sounds kinda like Chinese, doesn't it," he said as he excused himself to go the men's room. He held the Armani jacket over the front of his pants.

"I'll be right back," he said as he stood up.

He thought, can you imagine walking to the men's room at "21" and having to say, "Oh excuse me Madame," to some diamond encrusted lady as she stares at the front of your pants?

As I returned to the table, I didn't realize how long I'd taken. Sybil was standing alone waiting by the door, smoking her cigarette from the long silver holder. Everyone else had left.

"Michael, what took you so long? I told you we had to get back to the set." She looked angry as she glanced down at her Cartier watch. We went out the door and got into her limo.

"I just . . . "

"Never mind. I'm dropping you off at the Strassberg Institute. I want you to sign up and start today."

"But I don't have the . . . "

"Just tell them to charge it my account." She scribbled a little note on the back of her business card. "Here, just give them this. I think they know me there."

Before I knew it, the limo glided to the curb and let me out. I was being deposited in front of a non-descript little building in the village, just down the street from a seedy corner pizza parlor. I didn't even have one dollar on me and I was going to acting school.

"I'll pick you up here when I'm done at the studio. I'll be back about 8 or 9 tonight. I'll send Cecil in to let you know I'm here," she said out of the window as the limo started to pull away from the curb.

Sure enough at a quarter to nine, Cecil came to get me. I was totally absorbed watching an advanced class. A student was doing a scene from "Butterflies are Free" and you could swear he was really blind. But here was Cecil standing right in front of me, her driver's cap tilted forward on her head, the elaborate gold "S's" embroidered on her lapels.

I asked, "Could you just wait a few minutes, so I can see the actor finish his scene?"

"Never, and I mean never, keep Sybil waiting. You'd better leave immediately," she whispered. I was surprised she had such a low voice for such a pipsqueak of a girl.

So she could speak, after all. Those were the first words I'd ever heard her say. I left the room as quietly as possible, with Cecil right behind me.

CHAPTER III - Monday, August 4

Riverhead Correctional Facility

Sleeping on this thin mattress over slats is not what I was used to. Here I am at The Riverhead Correctional Facility out on Long Island. The morning before I went before a judge who set bail at one million dollars. Where the hell was I going to get that kind of money? And they're trying to pin Melody's murder on me too. She was only seventeen. Rape and murder. Eric and now Melody too. One million dollars. And I just turned twenty-five a few nights ago.

That night at Alan's house in the Hamptons turned into a real nightmare. It all keeps coming back to me, like a bad dream. Eric was chained up against the wall, his back bloody. Melody tried to run out of the door, but it was locked. She pounded on the door, screaming, "Someone, someone please let me out of here."

She was hysterical.

"Michael, relax, make yourself comfortable. You're going to be here for awhile"

"Alan, you're making a big mistake."

Melody just stood there at the thick padded door in a zombie-like state, staring at me.

"No, Michael, I'm not making a mistake. I think it's you and all those like you who make the mistake. You're the type that always wants something for nothing, you make no effort of your own. You just waltz in and try to waltz through life on someone else's back, on someone else's hard won efforts, on someone else's lifelong struggles, giving their blood, their sweat, yes even their tears."

Alan was leaning into my face with his boozy breath.

"But they mean nothing to you, their struggles, their tears, no, you care nothing for them. You care nothing for them because there is only yourself, your own dear precious carcass."

Alan tried to grab me but I pushed him away, and then with

no warning, he punched me right in the face. I lost my balance. The older man was upon me, as he and Alan grabbed my arms and pinned them back behind me. They pushed me over to the wall, next to Eric. I kicked at them as I struggled to get loose, but the two men were too strong to overcome. Each man firmly held an arm as they chained my wrists to the wall. Allan took a knife out of his pocket and slit my shirt and ripped it off.

Alan continued, screaming like a mad man right in my face, "All you do is take, eat, indulge yourself, you're nothing but a human compost machine, you're worthless human garbage."

I managed to kick Alan good and hard in the stomach before he could shackle my ankles. Then he punched me again, this time right on the mouth, making my lip bleed. Melody was all crumpled up sitting next to the door crying.

Alan started to calm down now that I was helpless and shackled to the wall. Alan looked at Eric and then at me, "That's all I ever have around me, the finest, the best that money can buy, if you know what I mean. I don't think you have any idea what you and your friend are going to be doing for me for the rest of the night, do you?"

Alan took a small vial out of his pocket, sprinkled some white power on the back of his hand and sniffed it. "Heroin, pure heroin. Takes a while to get used to it, but shortly everything will seem all right, then everything will be golden and nothing will seem to matter to you anymore." He poured more of the white power out and held it right under my nose. "Here take a sniff. All the things that torture you and bothered your brain and ripped at your heart and soul everyday, none of that will matter anymore. It all seems so insignificant and you wonder, why did I ever worry about that in the first place. Then you'll wonder why you never saw things like this before. This becomes the reality. And you'll never want to go back to that other horrible superficial reality again. That's why heroin is so addictive."

Alan sniffed more of the white power. "All the other reality does is make you suffer."

I snapped myself back from remembering that horrible night, but it kept running over and over again through my mind.

I remembered just a few short days ago I was getting picked up by Sybil in her limo after my first day at the Strasberg Institute in the village. She seemed annoyed that I had kept her waiting.

"So how did your first day go," Sybil asked as Michael slid into back seat of the limo beside her. She planted a long hot kiss on his mouth before he could even answer.

"To tell you the truth, I am tired, but I still feel great." He was going to mention that he hardly slept the night before, but he thought better of it. "I can't believe you're doing all this for me. I'll be forever grateful. Thank you, Sybil."

Michael felt a hard slap across his face.

"Never, ever say thank you to me, for anything Michael. Thank you's are for strangers, and let me tell you, we're going to be anything but strangers to each other."

Then she kissed him long and hard and deep. He was speechless.

He didn't think he'd ever been slapped before by a woman. Soon the limo pulled up to an ornate pre-war building on Park Avenue. Michael tried to retrieve all his Armani shopping bags as the trunk popped open, but the doorman beat him to it. They entered the lobby and got on an elevator that had art deco doors.

Sybil put in a code to open the elevator doors to the 19th floor. Her apartment was magnificent and huge. It took up the whole floor. It was furnished with lots of expensive looking antiques. Dinner was served by a maid in a black and white uniform in the large dining room high up overlooking Park Avenue. The city lights were twinkling beyond the tall windows and Michael could see the large expanse of Central Park. Dinner was just for the two of them. They were seated at opposite ends of a long dining room table. The walls were covered in dark red damask with a single row of small white bleached cattle skulls circling the room.

"How did the classes go today? Strasberg's the best."

"They interviewed me for about an hour, wanted to know everything about me. They showed me a video about the school, with Lee Strasberg himself talking, the head of the school. Do you think I'll get any lessons from the great man himself?"

"I don't think so, he's been dead for several years."

"Then I filled out a form. I didn't know what to put for my address so I left it blank."

"Put this address down."

"You mean I can stay here for awhile, with you?"

"Yes. Tell me more about the school?"

"There were photos all over the walls signed by all the famous actors who had been students there. I have to practice a scene from 'A Streetcar named Desire,' by Tennessee Williams for tomorrow."

"I knew him, before he died, choked to death in his hotel room right here in Manhattan. He was gay. I always wondered how he could write such fantastically charged scenes between men and women."

"I have to practice a scene, the one played by Marlon Brando."

"He must have loved watching Marlon play that part with his shirt off. I think you should practice your scene after dinner. I'll help you."

"You will? You don't have to. I'm supposed to meet someone after class tomorrow to practice the scene with, another student at her apartment. She's going to play Stella."

Sybil's eyes went dark. I wasn't sure what I had done.

"Michael, just finish your dinner without me. I have some paperwork to do." She shoved her chair back and left the room.

I didn't want to blow all this. I thought I was falling in love with her. I knew it and I couldn't help myself. She was so different. The maid came back in carrying a silver tray with a tiny white cup with the initial "S" on it in gold, half filled with espresso. There was a tiny lemon peel on the saucer. The maid opened a silver box for me. I had expected cigars, but they were hand rolled cigarettes. I took one out and the maid lit it with a blue lapis lighter, and then handed the lighter to me.

"A gift from Madame." She had a Spanish accent. She was short, had very dark hair pulled back in a bun, and no makeup.

As I puffed on one, I realized they weren't cigarettes at all, but pot, Mary Jane, marijuana and damn good stuff too, the best ever, better than what I grew behind my uncle's barn back in Missouri. I took a real deep drag and started to relax for the first time since I arrived in the city. Just as I put my feet up on the chair next to me, the maid said, "Let me show you to your room."

She led Michael down a long hallway lit by lamps extending out from the walls, ebony arms holding torch-shaped glass shades, past a library, past a card room, past a billiard room. He was disappointed Sybil didn't come back to join him.

The maid showed Michael to a small room with a black and white tiled floor, no rug, a single bed with a four poster metal frame, and no pictures on the walls. It looked like a monk's chambers. Then he noticed, there were no windows and the walls were covered in cork. The black silk comforter on the bed had a large initial "S" embroidered in gold in the center of it. There was a red terry cloth robe hanging from the back of the door. The maid closed the door behind her as she left.

He took off his Armani suit, his Armani loafers and the argyle socks and put on the robe. When he hung his suit in the closet, he found the other purchases of that afternoon already hanging there. He put on the red terry cloth slippers.

The other door was to a private bathroom and all the men's toiletries he could want were laid out on a glass shelf above the sink. There was a huge bottle of Safari cologne by Ralph Lauren in a crystal bottle, a razor with a mother of pearl handle. Nothing cheap here, he thought as he dabbed on the cologne. There was a stack of thick white towels, a large soap hanging by a rope from the shower head, still in its plastic wrapper. Michael took a long hot shower and totally lost track of time.

As he lay back on the bed with just a small towel over his

bronzed lean body, he felt a strange feeling of contentment. Here he was in New York, and for now anyways, nothing really mattered, except he was feeling so good, almost euphoric.

Just as he was about to doze off, he heard the door open. He thought it was the maid, but it was Sybil. She was wearing a black leather skin tight shirt that pushed her ample breasts up and a short black leather skirt. She wore long black leather boots with sky high stiletto heels. Her arms were covered in long black leather gloves with just her fingers showing out.

"Michael, I think you need some discipline."

He was so turned on by the sight on her, he tried to hold her as she sat down on the edge of his bed, but she pushed his hands away. Then she was on top of him, with her knee digging into his stomach. She had him turn over. She was holding a black leather riding crop and used it to tickle him between his legs and then back and forth over his buttocks. He was starting to get very aroused. She used the crop to smack the inside of his thighs with quick little snaps. He felt intense pleasure.

Before he even realized what she was doing, she was slipping his wrists into handcuffs and attaching them to the head posts, He couldn't move. He should have resisted, but he was curious to see what she was going to do next. He was beginning to get nervous as she put his ankles into shackles and attached them to the foot posts. Now he was spread eagled on his stomach and he couldn't move. Then smack, smack, smack on his naked buttocks, first lightly, then tingly. It gave him an odd sensation of pleasure. She used her black leather riding crop a bit harder across his back.

Then smack, smack, smack again and again on his naked buttocks, first lightly, then harder. He was surprised it actually felt good on his tough tanned skin. They felt like little stings and the slaps of a tough Japanese masseur. Then one was too hard and it stung his back.

"Sybil, stop, please stop." He wanted to get out of there, but his wrists and ankles were shackled. He wanted her to stop, he needed her to stop, but all he could do was twist from side to side, but still it was all strangely stimulating.

Suddenly she stopped and removed the handcuffs and ankle shackles. He rolled over onto his back. She put a blindfold over his eyes and mounted him. She pulled open the snaps on her shirt and rubbed her ample breasts against his chest. Then she sat up and rode him till he was senseless with pleasure. He tried to hold back from bursting forth. He tried to hold back with all his might. The heightened desire made the room seem to spin around. His orgasm was so intense, bursting forth again and again, like a gigantic fountain exploding. He could feel her vibrating again and again with him. It was the most fantastic orgasm he ever had. She moaned with pleasure as she came again and again.

He heard her walk to the door and heard the door close. He removed the blindfold and rubbed his wrists. He hated to admit it, he felt a strange peace like he never felt before. The sex was the most explosive, the most intense he ever had. Several minutes passed, he didn't know how long. Then he heard footsteps coming down the hallway.

He wondered if it was Sybil coming back to so something more unspeakable to him, with half wish, half dread. Then the door opened. He sat up. He was disappointed to see it was only the maid standing there in her black and white uniform. His mouth was as dry as the Sahara Desert. She handed him a goblet of ice cold water with a tiny mint leaf floating in it. He felt the pleasure of that water going down his throat. She poured more water into the goblet and he downed all that too. The maid told him to turn around and she put some kind of miracle salve on his back. Suddenly his back felt cool and the tingling sensation stopped.

The maid left the room. He looked at his back in the mirror. He could see a patchwork of fine lines, just red but no broken skin. Michael took another long drink of water straight from the pitcher. He was totally exhausted and fell into a long deep sleep.

CHAPTER 4 - Wednesday, July 30, Manhattan

When I woke up the next morning in Sybil's apartment, the maid was standing over me with a worried look on her face.

"Signor, I've been trying to wake you for five minutes." She looked down at her watch. "You have just enough time to get ready."

I tried to focus my eyes to see what she was trying to hand me.

"Please take your orange juice. It weel help you to wake up," she said in her heavy Spanish accent.

I finally managed to reach out and take the glass from her hand and saw her frowning at me. She was holding a small silver tray with a large bottle of aspirins on it.

"Please tell me your name. You've been so kind and I don't even know your name."

"Maria."

Michael felt some pain across his back and he remembered

the night before, the exquisite pain, the heightened pleasure, Sybil in that black outfit, the whip, the chains. He wondered what today would bring. He gratefully took the two aspirins Maria was holding out for him and swallowed them. She set down the tray and said, "Let me feex your back for you."

She took a tube of ointment out of her pocket and smoothed the ointment ever so lightly over his back. The cooling effect was immediate.

"Breakfast will be served for you in the dining room, but you better hurry. Do not shower today," she instructed, just use these." She handed him a stack of white wash cloths.

Will Sybil be joining me for breakfast?"

"Oh, no," Maria laughed, "Madame has already gone out. She left for the studio. They are already filming."

"Hell, what time is it? My first class was supposed to start today at nine."

"It's 9:15 right now," Maria said as she looked down at her big Timex watch.

"Shit," Michael said as he leapt out of bed before he realized he was totally naked. He grabbed his jeans and held them in front of him, "I guess I better hurry."

"A car will take you to the school as soon as you have your breakfast." She walked out of the room and closed the door behind her.

Here it was his first day and he was already missing his first class. "Hell, if I hurry, I can get there in time for the next class, the important one."

He quickly washed and slipped into his jeans and shirt. He thought they looked kind of funny with the Armani loafers. "I'll have to tell Sybil to get me a new pair of Nike's." He didn't want to put on his old worn down cowboy boots.

Michael hurried to the dining room and was almost blinded by the light streaming in through the large windows. The apartment was so high up he saw pigeons flying by. Some were trying to land on the ledges.

On the table was a silver coffee pot and a plate with a silver dome over it. He lifted it and found scrambled eggs, bacon and hash browns. Maria brought out fresh toast and apricot jam. He didn't realize how hungry he was as quickly devoured all of it. The white bleached animal skulls on the red walls seemed even more hideous with the bright morning light streaming in.

"The car is waiting downstairs in front of the building. You know the driver. Cecil will take you."

Michael took a last gulp of the hot coffee and bolted out of the heavy mahogany doors. The elevator seemed to take forever. It had dark wood paneling and an oriental rug on the floor. When the doors finally opened, he ran through the lobby almost knocking over a large oriental vase full of fresh flowers on a marble table. The vase would have tipped over if he had not caught it in time. The silver haired uniformed doorman gave him a disapproving look as he held the door open for him.

Cecil was there at the curb waiting for him. He slid into the back seat of the big black limousine. It was the first time he was there by himself. He was starting to feel important, and was thinking, if you can make it here, you can make it anywhere, just like the song said. He wanted to be an actor and everything that went with it. He admired the tall buildings as they whizzed by and thought, what better way to make it than to start at the top like this, living on Park Avenue.

Cecil interrupted his reveries, "Michael, you will be ready to be picked up at six today. Madame is taking you out for the evening. I believe it's your birthday."

"I forgot all about it. I'm turning twenty-five today. All the more reason why I've got to make this work. It has to work. I can never go back. Besides there's nothing to go back to. This is it, sink or swim."

Then I remembered I had the practice session with Melody after classes were over, the lovely girl I met when I signed up, the class I was racing to get to, the class we decided to take together. Beautiful sweet Melody, only seventeen and she seemed so innocent.

Cecil's harsh voice intruded on my vision of Melody playing Stella and kissing me as Stanley Kowalski.

"Michael, remember to be outside at six sharp."

"But Cecil, I can't. I have to practice a scene with a girl in my class. I'm supposed to be at her apartment at 7:00. We have to prepare a scene together for a reading for class the next day. It's really important."

"Michael, you don't seem to understand," her tone was firm. "You don't seem to know what is important."

"Cecil, I can't be there at six. That's all there is to it."

"Michael, you have to be there. You NEVER say 'no' to Sybil."

"But Cecil, we're got to prepare. They're going to let the best students go to the showcase Friday when the Broadway producers and scouts will be there. It could be my big chance."

"Michael, you must leave school at six promptly."

Yes, of course, how stupid of me, she was right. For a moment I almost forgot, without Sybil, there was no apartment, without Sybil, there was no school. They'll be other times, other opportunities, Michael tried to reason with himself.

"Yes, of course, I'm sure they have these readings all the time, and after all, it is my birthday. Time to celebrate." But what he was really thinking to himself was, next time he wouldn't miss out, no matter what.

Soon we were pulling up in front of the school. What was I going to say to Melody. How was I going to tell her. I'd make up some excuse or other.

I didn't realize how hard I slammed that car door as I got out of the limo.

"Watch the door, Michael. Well, you'll be here at six?"

"I'll be out here at six, exactly," as if she didn't already know.

"Good choice, Michael. I'll let Sybil know." She gave me a strange look and I blushed as I remembered the night before.

Was I dreaming or was Cecil standing at the door watching as Sybil used her riding crop across my back as I lay there naked chained to the bed?

As Cecil drove off, I realized I didn't have even one dollar on me for lunch or a drink. Then I felt something in the front right pocket of my jeans. It took it out and saw it was two twenty dollar bills. I guess Sybil thinks of everything.

As Michael entered the classroom, he heard the teacher telling the class of ten students, "Relive moments from your own life that relate to the scene. Relax, sit way back in the chair, further down, relax deeper to draw up those real experiences, those real emotions as if you were there again in your own past." I hurried over as quietly as I could to an empty seat next to Melody. She was flopped back, her eyes closed, her arms outstretched by her sides, just like a real angel.

The teacher, Harry, a good looking guy in his thirties, gave me a dirty look. "Relax, take a real deep breath, and again. Are you thinking of that moment? Are you reliving the moment? Are you there again? This is what is called the Method, to use your instrument, yourselves, your own real emotion from your own real experiences. This is what can make a powerful impact, not 'acting." Acting is when you impose a fake reaction, artificially. It has to be real to work. One famous actor said, when he starts 'acting' that's when he'll quit the profession. In other words, a real actor is one who never acts. He feels, he experiences, he calls forth his own real raw emotions."

Harry looked around the room at the students slumped in their chairs. "You can sit up now, open your eyes. I want you to yell, to really yell as loud as you can, to really let go. Loosen up that instrument, yell with all you've got. Don't be afraid to let go. Now!"

The whole class let out an ear-piercing yell.

Harry continued, "Now we're going to do what seems like a simple exercise. You're going to pour yourself that first cup of coffee in the morning from an imaginary coffee pot and you're going to drink or rather experience that first cup of coffee in the morning."

He looked around the classroom, "It sounds easy, but to be convincing, you will have to call up your sense memory of it being early in the morning, the feel of the cup, the smell of the coffee. You are barely awake, you have to call up that aroma, the feeling of that hot soothing liquid going down your throat. Your pleasure of the first taste, your reaction to a real event. You have to be convincing to your audience. This is what is called 'sense memory.'"

A fat wiseass guy in the back said, "Boy, that's sounds so complicated, why don't you just use real coffee."

"Bob, this is your basic training, your building blocks to calling up your own experiences. When you're reading your scene this afternoon, we'll see if you can call up your own experiences, your own real emotions. So we'll start with you, Bob. Go ahead, it's morning, have your first cup of coffee."

"No problem," Bob shot back.

Bob was really fat and said he was a truck driver, but wanted to quit to be an actor. Bob mentioned Rock Hudson and how he used to be a truck driver 'till he made it big. I hated to break it to Bob, but Rock Hudson was gay and died of AIDS.

Bob was a real comedian. He made believe he spilled the hot coffee on his foot and started hopping around the classroom. The teacher was not amused. Bob was probably going to be a great comedian and make it big on Saturday Night Live.

"Michael, you're next. And next time, try not to be late. It disrupts the class."

It seemed so silly, pantomiming, pouring air, drinking air. I did it as best I could, but Harry made me redo it three times.

"O.K. Karen, you're next."

Melody was looking at me like she wanted me. She whispered, "I'm looking forward to our practice session tonight."

Then before I knew it, Harry called lunch break.

"Melody, there's something I have to tell you. I can't make it tonight. My aunt is taking me out for a birthday dinner. I have to go, but we can practice during lunch. Let me buy us some pizza and we can find an empty classroom and practice there."

"But Michael, this is so important. We really need the whole evening to prepare. And nobody's going to be at my house to interrupt us 'till much later." She took my arm as we walked to the corner pizza place.

I felt terrible to see the hurt and disappointment on her face. "I'll make it up to you. There's a party at the Metropolitan Museum this Thursday night. Why don't you meet me there at nine. It's a special event, black tie."

"Don't I need a ticket to get in?"

"I'll get you one," I offered with no idea how I was going to do it, but I'd figure it out. Sybil was taking me.

When we returned to the school, we went up to the third floor and found a large deserted room. After wolfing down the pizza and coke, we started to kiss, though we couldn't seem to stop and before I knew what I was doing, we were on the floor. I was on top of her tearing off her clothes and she was letting me. She did try to stop me at first, and then I knew why. She was a virgin. This was her first time. But then again, she wasn't really resisting.

"I didn't mean to do that, to start this. I just couldn't help myself." I heard myself apologizing to her. But she was just smiling at me. She was so young and beautiful.

"It's my first time. I didn't want you to know."

Just as I was tucking my shirt back in my jeans, several students started walking into the room talking to each other. Lunch break was over. Melody and I hurried downstairs to our class. Harry told us to review our scenes.

"You're going to do your scene today, reading from the book. But tomorrow, you're going to do it from memory, act out the scene with your partner.

CHAPTER 5 - Monday, August 4

Riverhead Correctional Facility

After the judge set my bail at one million dollars, I was transferred to the Riverhead Correctional Facility, about a half an hour way. After entering on the prison bus through tall barb wired fences, manacled hand and foot, and then going through processing, I found myself sitting on the edge of my bed in a cell in a daze. I was lost in thought at the hopelessness of my situation. I couldn't believe bail was set at one million dollars. The judge said I was considered a flight risk plus the seriousness of the charge. A public defender was going to be assigned to my case.

There just didn't seem to be any hope for me. But maybe I still have a chance. Sure, a chance against Alan. Right. Fat chance. Like finding an ice cube in hell. He's probably bought and paid for everyone in this town already. They're not going to listen to me, a hayseed blown in here from nowhere. No money, no connections, nothing. I'm really in this one all by myself. To get mixed up with these people. I should have stayed where life was simple, where people were simple. They said what they meant and they did what they said. None of this twirling and twirling into lies, lives built on lies and deceit. I havn't heard one word from Sybil yet. She was my one phone call, but the maid Maria answered it and said "Madame is out." I told her where I was and that I needed her help.

The guard brought a big black guy to my cell. No more single room. He sat down on the other bed.

"What are you in here for?" I asked. "Might as well try to make conversation to pass the time."

"Armed robbery."

"What's your name?"

"Herman. O.K., you wanna talk. What are you in here for?"

"Murder, maybe double murder." Michael took a deep breath, "But I didn't do it."

"That's what they all say."

"It was a grisly sex slay murder, a guy just about my age. I was there when it happened, but I didn't do it. I tell you I'm being framed."

"Hey, how'd you get in this mess anyways?"

It all started with a woman. Actually two women."

"That figures. Why don't you tell me about it. Anyways, it'll pass the time, and that's something we got plenty of in here."

"Well, I was getting in heavy with this woman Sybil, a film producer, living in her apartment on Park Avenue, when I met this girl Melody. That's when all this trouble began. Now they're trying to pin her murder on me too. She was just seventeen."

"Go ahead. Tell me the story."

"We were in the same acting class together at Strasberg's in the village. We were doing a scene together, and it was my turn to read. The instructor, Harry, told me to take off my shirt. I told him I couldn't, but he insisted, saying that was how Marlon Brando did it and if it was good enough for Brando, that's how I was going to do it too. I didn't want to argue with him, so I took my shirt off. The class gasped when they saw my back. Melody looked sick. There was a little cross work of pink lines all across my back.

Then I really got into the scene, screaming "Stella, Stella," as I fell to my knees before Melody. I yelled, "Sybil, Sybil" as I flashed back to the night before when she held me her prisoner of pleasure and pain.

There was a moment of silence. Then the teacher told me to go back to my seat. He paused and said, "Michael, that was quite good. Yes, really quite good actually. I'm very impressed with you for a new student. But don't forget to memorize the playwright's words. The name is Stella."

After class, Melody pleaded with me one more time to go with her to practice at her apartment, but I told her I couldn't. I finally had to tell her it wasn't my aunt, but a film producer and I couldn't get out of it.

All she said was, "Oh Michael, I want to believe you."

I had to hurry to meet Cecil at the curb at six, but I did manage to get Melody's number. I rushed out onto the street before Melody could see me slip into the limo.

Sybil was in the back seat, "I've got a lot of surprises planned for you tonight." She handed him one of the Armani bags. "Here change into this."

The cars were crawling slowly along during rush hour, but he had to change in the back seat. Good thing the windows were tinted, he thought to himself. As the car wound up Fifth Avenue., he took off his jeans and slipped into a beige Armani suit. He combed his hair as best he could. As they got out of the limo, he saw the big chrome letters, "Fortunoff" across the top of the building on Fifth Avenue.

Sybil led him a counter filled with dazzling gold jewelry.

"Let's see," Sybil searched the case as the young salesgirl came over to help her. "Yes, let's try this one." Sybil pointed to a heavy gold chain.

"Oh yes, that's a very beautiful one, an Italian design. Would your son like to try it on?"

The attractive salesgirl gave Michael a flirtatious look.

Sybil looked annoyed, but she didn't miss a beat. "That's not my son."

The salesgirl looked embarrassed when she figured out Sybil's meaning from the way she said it. "Oh, I'm sorry, of course not. Here let me help him try it on." She came around the counter and fastened the heavy gold chain at the back of Michael's neck. She held up a mirror for him to see it.

Michael admired himself in the mirror, "Yes, it's perfect."

"Then, we'll take it. Leave it on. Try this on too."

Sybil picked out a heavy gold bracelet to match. The salesgirl took it out of the case and Sybil put it on Michael's wrist herself.

"And now, so you'll never be late for me, let's pick out a watch."

Michael could only nod in agreement. He had never expected anything like this.

"Let's try on this Gucci." Sybil picked out a wonderful Gucci with a black face and gold roman numerals. It had a black lizard band. She strapped the watch onto Michael's wrist. He didn't know what to say. He was forbidden to 'thank you,' so he just looked at her with gratitude and love, love and longing to hold her, to take her into his arms and make mad passionate love to her, to make love like a wild animal with no constraints, with wild total abandon, Michael thought to himself.

"Sybil, I don't know what to say. These are all so wonderful."

The salesgirl handed her the sales receipt, "That will be two thousand three hundred dollars."

Sybil didn't even look at it. She just handed the girl her charge card. She signed quickly, as if it didn't even matter to her.

"And now for dinner. I have a special treat for you.'

Cecil whisked them just a few blocks away and let them out in front of Petrossian's. It was a funny looking corner building with an ornate stone facade. There were two dragons with crowns on their heads carved into the stone over the door. After they were seated, the only thing Michael saw on the menu was caviar and smoked fish. Michael had never eaten caviar before.

Sybil ordered for both of them, the best, Russian Beluga from the Caspian Sea. and a bottle of Dom Perignon champagne.

The waiter uncorked the bottle with a loud pop, the cork landing skillfully right into the linen napkin he was holding.

"Here's a toast to us, and to you on your birthday, Michael. Happy Birthday."

They toasted each other, and he thought this was the best, the driest champagne he ever had. The waiter then served the caviar still in its small glass jar and set it down on ice in a silver bowl. He looked down at little grey specks, fish eggs, roe, and triangular pieces of golden brown toast. Michael watched as

Sybil layered the caviar on the toast, sprinkling chopped pieces of egg white, diced onion and the round green capers. She popped the whole thing in her mouth. He wanted to reach over and kiss her, but he tried to behave himself. They were in a restaurant, after all. And she was wearing red lipstick. He tried the caviar, doing exactly as she had done. He was expecting to hate it, but he didn't. It was delicious and he wolfed it down on the dainty little pieces of toast. He lifted his champagne glass toward Sybil, "To you Sybil, and the best darn birthday I ever had."

Michael looked down at the beautiful gold bracelet and the Gucci watch she had bought him and his eyes got misty. This was so unlike him, to be so emotional, but he felt he was falling in love with her. Melody was like a toy, an intrigue, and he didn't want to hurt her, but it could never get serious. This was serious with Sybil and it scared him. He'd never been with one girl for more than three months and that was his limit. But somehow he wanted this to be different. It wasn't all the presents or the limo or the apartment on Park Avenue. He felt she really cared about him. He never really had that before. But a nagging thought kept running through his mind. He had promised to call Melody. He excused himself from the table and hurried downstairs to the restroom where he found a pay phone. He dialed Melody's number, which he had memorized by heart.

"Melody, this is Michael."

"I know who you are, silly. I thought you were never going to call. So how's your big date with the movie producer going?"

"Look, I can't really talk right now. I just wanted to see how you're doing, you know, after what happened this afternoon."

"I'm great. Can you come over after your meeting?"

"No, but don't forget about the Met, tomorrow night, at nine. I have to get there early."

Just then he saw Sybil winding her way down the stairs.

Michael quickly hung up the phone, hoping Sybil didn't see him and hurried up the stairs towards her.

"Wonderful dinner." He was so flustered he didn't know what else to say.

"See you back at the table," she shot him a suspicious look as she headed towards to ladies room.

Soon she was back at the table and seated herself.

"Drink up, Michael. We're going to a club downtown."

My curiosity was stirred as Cecil whisked us downtown, all the way down Broadway. Especially beautiful was the top of the Chrysler Building, wearing its arches, all lit up like a space age crown. In the limo, Sybil handed Michael a large gift-wrapped package.

"Happy Birthday, Michael. Go ahead, open it."

"Not more gifts. I don't deserve all this Sybil." He carefully opened the package, not wanting to ruin the beautiful silver paper. He took out a leather shirt and leather pants and two leather wrist bands with a metal ring attached to each one.

"Here, put these on." The leather pants fit perfectly, too perfectly. Sybil helped him strap the leather band on each wrist.

Soon Cecil was driving down a trash littered street in the heart of Chelsea, past the infamous Chelsea Hotel where artists, models and heroin addicts lived. Sybil told him Warhol filmed "Chelsea Girls" there, with all his transvestites and pretty boys.

Trash spilled out of metal cans and there was a stray dog trying to find his dinner in one of them. There was a warm light drizzle as they stepped out of the limo. A doorman with a leather motorcycle cap and a small ring through his right nostril waved them in. Sybil handed the girl at the entry desk an invitation. They walked down a long dark black corridor, then came upon a room full of people, men and women, straight and gay, punks and people in business suits, and people wearing leather. On a large stage was a live band, three guys and a girl lead singer playing heavy metal music booming out over gigantic loud speakers, so loud the walls vibrated. They were playing "Hot in the City," a Billy Idol song. The girl had bright pink and orange hair sticking straight up.

A guy wearing only underwear, no shirt, no shoes or socks, came crawling on all fours up to Sybil. He fawningly asked, "Please let me lick your boots." She shoved him away with her Laboutin as he started to lick it.

Then Michael noticed at the back of the room a huge wheel, like a gigantic wheel of fortune. There was a muscular guy in a g-string strapped to it and the wheel was slowly turning around. It looked like a crazy Leonardo da Vinci drawing. Only there was a real human in it. The wheel was slowly going round and round, the guy turning over and over.

A girl with a tall funny looking black hat like a crushed version of the Mad Hatter's, came up and greeted Sybil with a big hug and kissed her first on one cheek and then the other. "She's the hostess. She gives these parties."

The girl said, "Try to stick around. Billy Idol's supposed to show up later."

We went up to the bar to order drinks. The bartender had a shaved head and a safety pin through one of his cheeks.. He wore leather pants and an open leather vest showing his hairy chest. When the bartender turned around to fix a drink, Michael noticed the back portion of the pants was missing and his bare buttocks were showing out.

Sybil walked us to a back room. A tall transvestite was the gate keeper. His features were frighteningly beautiful, with his long dark hair and perfect make up.

"O.K., you can come in," he said in an English accent. He parted a black curtain. On a wall at the back of the room was a guy being handcuffed to large rings above his head. He was standing facing the wall. His wrist bands were just like the ones Sybil had given me. The transvestite selected a black whip from the wall and handed it to a man in a three piece grey suit.

Sybil saw Michael was not comfortable being there, afraid he was going to be next.

"I'd really like to go now, can't we just get out of here."

"O.K. Michael, if you insist. It is your birthday."

&&&&&&&&&&&&&&&

That night, back at her Park Avenue Apartment, Sybil let Michael make love to her in her bedroom, a large and surprisingly feminine room, all ruffles and lace. He forgot all about the evening and lost himself in her warm comforting body and made love to her the way he wanted to, soft and tender and she seemed to be yielding to him. And that was the best birthday present of all.

CHAPTER 6 - Thursday, July 31, Manhattan

I was barely awake and found myself feeling very content in Sybil's enormous bed. She was already dressed and just finishing arranging her hair in the mirror on her dressing table. There were about thirty flasks of all kinds of perfumes on it. She came over to the bed and kissed me.

"Good morning, Michael. Tonight's the masquerade ball at the Museum, a benefit for the Costume Institute. There's going to be some people there I want you to meet. Cecil will drive you to St. Laurent to get fitted for a tux. Then she'll take you to your classes. You will be picked up at 7 P.M. exactly. There's a buffet at the Museum for the benefactors, a private party before the other guests arrive. We shall arrive together."

I tried to grab her to get her back into bed, but she laughed. "No, Michael, not now. I'll see you at seven."

She left the room. He lazed in bed a few minutes longer. Then he got up, put on his robe and walked over to the dressing table. He looked at himself in the mirror.

"I do feel older today. Twenty-five. But I sure don't feel any wiser."

He looked at the Gucci watch he still had on. It was only 7:30.

"Classes don't start 'til nine. I guess I'll miss that first class again, diction. Have to get my tux, Sybil's orders. Besides, I have to find an invitation for Melody," he said to himself.

Michael started snooping around Sybil's little writing desk in her bedroom. Nothing was on it, just some letters. He quietly opened the draw. Checkbook, cigarettes, green malachite lighter, an uncashed check from one of the studios for $50,000. Nice, to be able to let a check like that sitting around, he thought. Then, there it was, two invitations. He quickly took one and slipped it into the pocket of his robe, just in time before Maria entered the room.

"You should get back to your room now and get ready. Breakfast is being prepared." Maria looked at him suspiciously, but she didn't say anything more.

I was happy. I had it, the invitation for Melody. My spirits started to soar as I dressed for the wonderful day that lay ahead.

Breakfast was fabulous, fresh squeezed orange juice, a pile of thin pancakes, real maple syrup, little sausages, applesauce and rich dark coffee.

I took the elevator down, but today, I took my time as I casually walked across the lobby. The doorman tipped his hat and said, "Your driver is waiting for you, sir."

Yes, he addressed me as "Sir" as he held the door open for me. I was starting to really be a part of this lifestyle, a lifestyle I definitely could get used to. Cecil seemed a bit nicer today too, less formal.

"Good morning, Michael. Our first stop is Yves St. Laurent on Madison. You go in and get fitted. I'll wait for you in the car. They'll be expecting you."

A salesgirl unlocked the door when she saw me standing outside. The store had opened early especially for me. The girls brought out three tuxes and held them up. I picked the white one with the double breasted jacket, a light blue shirt with the old fashioned turned down collar, a royal blue cummerbund and a matching blue bow tie. The tailor came out and took all the measurements.

"The suit will be ready for you at 5:00 today."

"Cecil . . . ," I started to say as entered the limo . . .

"I know, the suit will be ready at five."

The class was already in progress. I entered as quietly as I could. Harry was giving instructions to the students who were stretched out in their chairs, their eyes closed, just like yesterday.

"You are each to think of an animal and try to visualize in your mind how the animal looks, how it moves, how it sounds, how it thinks, how it feels. You are to become that animal, be the animal. Not how it acts from outside to the observer. You must actually enter the psyche of that animal."

What was I going to be a lion, a bear, a snarling panther? I thought to myself.

The first student, Marvin, chose to be a lion. He crawled around on all fours, roaring, clawing at the air, snarling. I thought he was quite good, actually.

Then came Karen as a cat, purring, walking around. She came over to me and rubbed up against my leg. She was really good, but more like a sexy woman than a cat.

Oh, no, Bob was next. What was he going to be? He started hopping around the room. He was a fucking kangaroo, a fat kangaroo, rubbing his two little fat hands together. Now I knew for sure that guy's going into comedy. The teacher didn't like his performance at all.

"No, no, no Bob. That is exactly what I mean. You're just doing the externals. I don't see you being a kangaroo at all."

Howard was really good as a chimpanzee, jumping up on a chair, shrieking, scratching under his arms, moving his head from side to side with darting eyes. He was the most convincing so far. It was kind of scary. Just for a moment, you really thought Howard had turned into a chimpanzee. He had transformed himself.

"Very good, Howard. Now Michael, what about you. What are you going to be? Just show us."

Before I knew it I was down on all fours, looking around. Then I started to bark, just like a real dog. I started sniffing at the girls' feet, their skirts, and howled, a long strange howl.

"O.K., good Michael." Harry looked at the big clock on the wall. "O.K., that's it for now, lunch break. Be back here in one hour."

Melody came over to me, "Michael, why did you hang up on me like that last night?"

She looked so fragile, so wounded, like she was about to burst out crying. I couldn't stand that. I wanted to scoop her up in my arms and just hold her.

"Melody, I'm so sorry. I didn't realize it sounded like that."

"Well, it really wasn't very nice and it hurt my feelings."

I almost forgot. I was her first lover, and it just happened yesterday afternoon.

"This might cheer you up. Here's the invitation I promised you." Michael took the invitation out of his pocket. "It's kind of formal. I hope you have something to wear."

She smiled at Michael and took the invitation. "I know what I'll be wearing, a blue satin dress, floor length, with red sequins and matching red shoes. The one I wore to my prom."

"That sounds beautiful, Melody," even though Michael thought it all sounded ghastly.

"Will you pick me up, Michael? You know I live way out in Queens, so maybe we can meet somewhere else."

"Melody, I'm going to have to meet you at the museum."

"O.K., I guess. I'll meet you there."

"Oh, I forgot to tell you. It's a masquerade ball, so be sure to bring a mask."

He had told her nine because he felt by then the place would be packed.

The last class was the monologue from Hamlet the "To be or not to be" speech. But before he knew it, it was seven o'clock. The class was running over. He had to leave right away. Michael slipped out as quietly as he could and found Cecil parked out front. Sybil was in the back seat. She greeted him and handed him the Yves St. Laurent tux. He quickly changed into it as they sped uptown to the Metropolitan Museum.

The Museum was a very large imposing building spread out along Fifth Avenue, bordering on Central Park. There were majestic fountains shooting high up on both sides of the grand entrance staircase. There was a long stream of limos waiting in line to unload their passengers. All the men were in black tuxedos and all the women had on long gowns with tons of jewelry. Members of the press were standing there popping flashbulbs as the guests got out of their limos.

So this was it., the rich and powerful of New York. And here I was, just a little ol' farm boy mixing in with them. Some were quite recognizable, a Kennedy here and there, a newscaster from T.V., a real estate wheeler and dealer and his wife. He knew he should recognize more of them, but he couldn't remember who they were. Most of them had no importance at all, other than they just plain had money, lots of it, and got it through one method or another. They either made it, robbed it, married it, or were born into it.

Sybil looked stunning in her gold lame gown, off one shoulder, with an incredible diamond necklace and long diamond earrings. She was glittering so much, I almost didn't know what to say. I had never seen her like that and, well, it made me feel a little awkward. We entered a room with a huge skylight which held an ancient Egyptian temple. Soon we were standing around drinking champagne and Sybil became quite chatty and sociable with some of the guests she seemed to know. Then she led me around, holding my arm, showing me off I guess, introducing me to this one and that one. I had to admit it, I looked damned good in my Yves St. Laurent tuxedo. It turned out to be a perfect fit.

"Michael, did you know this temple was removed stone by stone from Egypt after the dam broke, the Aswan Dam, and it was submerged under the flooded area. It's called the Temple of Dendur."

She told me this as we were walking over toward Alan, who was standing by the entrance to the Temple. "I want you to be especially nice to him tonight."

"Why tonight, Sybil?"

"I can't tell you everything. But you know he's head of development at the studio that's financing my film."

Alan stepped toward us and took my hand, "Michael, nice to see you again."

I wasn't sure I liked the way Allan grasped my hand. There was something uncomfortable about it, something I didn't like. It was too warm, too friendly, or was it just my overactive imagination. Alan finally let go when he spotted Annize. "Look there's Annize. I wonder who that new young guy is she's with. She always finds them, doesn't she?"

Then I saw her floating across the room towards me. Since Sybil had been walking ahead of me, she didn't seem to notice. It was Melody in her blue gown with red sparkles wearing her mask. I had to head her off. She could never, I mean never, be allowed to meet Sybil. Sybil was busy talking to Alan about some new project, so I excused myself "to go to the men's room."
I don't think they noticed me as I quickly weaved through the crowd toward Melody.

I steered her to the next room, which had exhibits in glass cases of dead mummies.

99

"Melody, you look breathtaking." It was cool in there, temperature controlled, to preserve the mummys, all those dried out wrapped up ancient Egyptians. It was kind of spooky.

"Somehow it doesn't seem right, to have dead people dug up from their graves, excavated out of the pyramids, to be put on public display," Melody observed as she looked into several of the cases. "This place is so gruesome."

"I just wanted to get you alone, all to myself. When you're around, I don't see anything but you." Michael walked Melody over into a corner of the room, bent over her and gave her a long kiss.

"Michael, I didn't know you were so romantic."

"I wish I could whisk you away from here on a magic carpet and spend about three eternities making love to you."

"Michael, I know you don't mean it."

"I don't even know what I'm saying. I think you're spinning some kind of enchanted spell over me tonight."

Just then, I noticed it was Annize leading her new boyfriend into the room to look at the mummys. I turned my back just in time so they couldn't see it was me.

Annize was saying, "Did you know they used an instrument with a hook on the end of it to actually pull the brains out through their nose as part of the embalming process? You know, so as to not cut or mess up their faces."

"I think plastic surgeons should try that on some of their clients," her boyfriend chimed in.

"Probably improve their I.Q.s," Annize laughed.

I walked Melody to the next room, hoping Annize didn't notice it was me.

"How terrible, did they really do all that stuff?" Melody asked.

"Oh yes, and then they put their organs into different jars that had different animal heads on them. A heart in one, the liver in another.

"I can't stand anymore of your embalming talk."

I peeked into the other room and saw that Annize and her boyfriend had left. "Thank heavens they left."

"Why do you know them?"

"No," I lied. "What they were saying was making me sick too. Let's go downstairs to see some of the costumes. That's what this benefit is about, isn't it."

Then I remembered my first night with Sybil in the limo and how she sent me up to Annize's apartment just like that, like some cheap gigolo. It made my face turn red to think I was so stupid then.

We went down the escalator hand in hand, as I kept a look-out for Sybil. When we got down there, I was surprised to see Alan looking at one of the old Chanel gowns.

"Michael, look at this one here, the lines, the grace." He put his arm around my shoulder. "If only today's designers could capture that look, that elegance. "But," he sighed, "that was a different era, a different time." He took a sip of his champagne.

He took Michael's hand, "Listen my boy, if you want some good advice, and I hear you're trying to enter the profession as an actor, don't rely on just one person. In other words, don't put all your eggs in one basket, because, you know, they might get broken." Then he laughed, "You know what I mean."

"Sure, Alan, good advice." Michael paused. "Let me introduce you to a friend of mine, from the acting school, and a very good little actress. Melody, I'd like you to meet Alan, the man responsible for many film projects getting made."

I didn't know what else to do. Maybe he wouldn't tell Sybil. He seemed pleased to meet Melody, and showed some interest in her.

"Oh, very pleased to meet you Alan." I was surprised to see Melody falling all over herself.

"By the way, did Sybil tell you I'm giving a party at my apartment tonight right after this dreadfully boring affair? I'm just three buildings down from here, on Fifth. I'm sure Sybil's taking you to it anyways."

"I don't know anything about it." I sure didn't want Alan mentioning Sybil in front of Melody. She looked upset.

"Michael, you naught boy," he said as glanced at Melody. This get together tonight is not going to be your liking, Melody, just a bunch of old fuddy duddies lifting their sniffters. But Saturday night, I'm having a real bash at my house out in the Hamptons. I'm sure you'd like that one much better. Why don't you come out to that one. Here's the address." He handed Melody his calling card. "It's at the beach. We're all very casual out there."

Melody looked at Michael, waiting for his answer.

"That's where we go to get away from this pressure cooker. Melody, why don't you come out Saturday and stay at my house for the weekend?"

Before I could say anything, Melody had accepted, "Oh, Alan, I'd love to come to your party Saturday and stay over, but just for one night. "

"Splendid, "Alan seemed pleased.

Melody glanced down at her watch. "As for tonight, I have to get going or I'm going to miss my train back out to Queens."

"Why don't I have my driver take you out there"

"No, no bother. It'll be quicker this way. See you at class tomorrow, Michael," she said as she started to walk toward the escalator. "And see you Saturday night, Alan. Thanks for the invitation."

She disappeared none too soon up the escalator, just as Sybil came bearing down on us, stepping off the down escalator. "What are you two so busy discussing? And where the hell have you been anyways, Michael? I've been looking all over for you."

I went to the men's room, Sybil, and when I came out I couldn't find you and I ran into Alan, who insisted I look at all these fabulous gowns from another time. I thought maybe you would be down here, too."

Whew, that was a close one. I just hope Alan doesn't say anything. I really gotta be more careful in the future, Michael thought, as his heart started racing from the near disaster.

CHAPTER 7 - Thursday, July 31, Manhattan

Alan's apartment was magnificent. Some people really knew how to live in New York. His living room was twice the size of Sybil's, with breathtaking views of Central Park. It had a huge terrace planted with trees and all sorts of heavenly scented flowers. Some of them were gardenias. You could see right into the glass pyramid enclosing the Temple of Dendur, which was all lit up against the night sky. There was a grand piano in Alan's living room, and someone was playing the Cole Porter tune, "Night and Day."

Just a dozen people had been invited. A uniformed butler was carrying a silver tray of hot hors d'oeuvres and a maid was serving drinks. Annize was there, but after a short time she said her thank you's to Allan, glanced at her boyfriend and laughing, said she had more important things to do. Then a few more people left.

"Thank heavens we finally got rid of all those boors," Allan said as he sat back in a big dark green easy chair and removed his bow tie and cufflinks. The maid brought him a brandy in a big snifter. Alan was chatting with a tall blond, the same woman who had been at the club the night I met Sybil. She was very elegant, wearing a 1920's style chartreuse cocktail dress, with Art Deco jewelry and seemed to be in her mid thirties.

Sybil took my hand and led me to a billiard room. She closed the door and locked it from the inside. It had green velvet walls lined with photographs of horses burdened with flowers in the winner's circles at Hialeah, Saratoga, Longchamps, Churchill Downs. There was an antique billiard table and a long comfortable sofa in paisley green with big pillows across the back. I was beginning to feel woozy after the long day and all those drinks, so I plopped down on the sofa. I heard flamenco music coming from the next room, the kind they do those crazy Spanish dances to, when a couple stamp their feet on the floor and whirl about getting closer and closer to each other.

Sybil sat down beside me and handed me a long thin pipe. "Are you ready to try something different. It's called opium. The drug of forgetfulness, of sensuousness."

"Sybil, you know I'm becoming yours and whatever you say, whatever you want me for, I want to do it."

She handed Michael the long thin pipe. It had a small black ball in it. He took a few long drags and soon everything looked and felt wonderful. The notes of the music suddenly became objects and he could actually feel them dancing on his skin. They were dancing all over him, they were caressing him, kissing him.

"Michael, come sit on the billiard table," Sybil laughed. "Now let's take off your clothes,"

I removed all my clothes and soon my beautiful new St. Laurent tux was on the floor. Sybil had me lay down right on the billiard table, as I sunk further into a golden haze. I felt my whole body needed sex. The opium made every pore want sex and my whole body vibrated with sexual energy. Soon I forgot about the people in the next room, as I laid back and let Sybil do whatever she wanted with me. She bent over and kissed me on the mouth. I don't know why but I bit her on her lip.

"Now, that's a very bad boy Michael. I thought you were mine, to do with as I pleased. That's right, isn't it? It's what you said."

She slipped a blindfold on me.

"Well then, silly boy, I'd like to put my mark on you. Do you agree?"

"Sybil, I am yours, to do with whatever you want. Yes, I would like to wear your mark."

Sybil opened the door and called in the tall blond woman. She came over and put rubbing alcohol all over Michael's right chest.

"Hold still, don't move," she said. She took a needle and pierced his nipple so quickly he didn't even know what was happening except for one sharp stab of pain. Then she inserted a small gold hoop through the hole.

"It bears my initial, Michael, 'S,' and now you belong to me, to do with as I wish."

The tall blond woman left the room and closed the door behind her. Then Sybil mounted Michael and rode him on the green billiard table. He lost all track of time. He just knew this was where he wanted to be, where he had to be, and when he couldn't hold back any longer, he just came and came and came and the throbbing orgasm seemed to go on forever.

CHAPTER 8 - Friday, August 1, Manhattan

I woke up with a vicious headache and found Sybil in my arms. We had fallen asleep on the big sofa in Allan's billiard room. It was very early in the morning. The light streamed in through the French windows past the heavy green drapery. It seemed no one else in the household was up. I could see the reservoir to the north. It looked like a big blue lake with the sunlight glistening on it.

Sybil gestured for me to be very quiet. We dressed and slipped out of the apartment. We jumped into a lone cab plying Fifth Avenue. I had never seen New York so deserted of people and cars.

We got back to Sybil's place to get ready for the day. It was Friday and this was the big day Melody and I were going to read in front of the Broadway producers. I still couldn't believe it, but Harry had chosen us with about twenty other students out of the whole school to read that very afternoon.

I showered and looked down at Sybil's ring piercing my right nipple. I ran my finger around the small gold hoop and felt her initial "S" engraved on it. I thought this was a strange place to wear a ring, but that's the way she was, nothing she ever did was usual. And certainly nothing was boring around her, I was certain of that. Now I wanted her all the time, she was so stimulating, so erotic. I couldn't stop thinking of her and last night. I had consented to be hers, to do with as she wished and that's exactly what she did.

I finished dressing and was about to leave my room when Maria came in and asked where I was going.

"Maria, this is my big day. I'm going to Strasberg's to read for a part in a play, a play on Broadway. Can you believe it, my first professional reading. Just wish me luck."

"Michael, you can't go today."

"What!" I wanted to scream. But it just came out softly. "What do you mean? I have class today, and this is an important reading. It's for Broadway. I have to go. My first big break is about to happen, I just know it."

"Michael, its Friday. And on this Friday, Madame is leaving at noon to go out to her house on the beach in East Hampton. Oh, you'll love it there. It's so beautiful."

"What about the filming, the filming at the sound stage. Isn't she filming there today?" I was getting panicky. "She can't be leaving today, of all days."

"Oh, they're not filming here today. When they continue filming on Monday, they're going to be filming out there, on Long Island for the rest of the movie. You know, location shooting. They're finished here."

"But I can't go. What about the school."

"Its August and nobody stays in the city in August. Madame is spending the entire month of August at her house in East Hampton. I believe she said she's taking you with her. I'm in the process of closing down the apartment. You'll find a suitcase in the closet. You should pack all your things, except the toiletries. You'll find others out there."

"Do you go too?"

"Yes, of course. Madame could never do without me."

I sat down on the bed, a bit bewildered. I had to go with her, of course. I was going to the Hamptons for the month of August. Well, it wasn't all that bad. New York was getting pretty disgusting anyways. The foul smells of the city were really getting intolerable, especially to this farm boy's sensitivities. You had to hold your nose whenever you walked by a gutter or a curb, or the piled up trash rotting on the sidewalks. Especially to be avoided were all the subway grates that whisked foul air up from the caverns below.

Now, come to think of it, this could be really great, the Hamptons in August. I guess it doesn't get any better than that. I could go back to acting classes in September and get another chance.

"Maria, did you say a house on the beach?"

"Oh, yes, a big house, right on the beach."

Maria left the room. I went to the closet and found a suitcase, an old Louis Vuitton. Nothing shabby about the way Sybil did things. Always the best, top cabin as she liked to say. I did as Maria said and packed all my clothes. I wondered if Melody would go to the party at Alan's house tomorrow night. I half hoped she would come and half dreaded it. I wondered what she would think when I didn't show up for class this morning. I would call her the first chance I got. Yes, I did want her to come out to the party. I had to see her again. Nothing would happen to her. She wasn't part of this, the mad ride I was on. Of course, she would be angry that I wasn't there for the reading today for the Broadway producers. Maybe she could get some one else to read with her.

In the car ride out to Long Island, we ran into terrible Friday afternoon traffic. Sybil lost her temper when we got caught in the long line of bumper to bumper cars on the Long Island Expressway.

"Michael, you're not getting it yet. But I'm sure you will. Cecil has been telling me about all the resistance you've been putting up to complying with my requests. By the way, who were you calling the other night at Petrossians?"

"I was calling my Aunt out in Missouri. I thought she would start worrying about me."

"Well, how's your aunt then?"

"Oh, she's fine. I hadn't called her since I left her at the apartment she rented in St. Louis. They're waiting to collect on the disaster insurance from the flood, but nobody knows how long that's going to take."

"Sybil looked skeptical, "Then why did you hang up when you saw me."

"Oh, we were just finished talking, that's all. I never have much to say to her anyways. And I didn't want to keep you waiting."

I was good at improvising as I went along. I just wondered if she was buying it. I hoped I wasn't turning red like I usually did when I was lying.

"You don't mind, do you, about leaving school?"

"No, Sybil. Whatever you want, that's what I want."

"Good."

"Anyways, I can go back to Strasberg's in September?"

Sybil didn't answer my half statement, half question. She seemed distracted.

Maria sat in the front seat with Cecil who never said a word. Finally we crept across the Shinnecock Canal. We were at the beginning of the Hamptons and it was truly beautiful with the tall reeds, the sand dunes. The quaint little New England towns had their neatly shingled houses with their bright white trim. Except for the long line of cars winding their way down the double lane road, it looked like paradise. Then we passed a huge overgrown cornfield that reminded me of back home. Black crows were circling overhead.

When we entered the town of East Hampton, it looked just like a storybook. There was an old grey shingled windmill that looked straight out of Holland. There were big tall weeping willows drooping over a pond. Two white swans were gliding along and pecking at whatever lurked in the water.

Cecil drove us straight to Sybil's place, a very modern glass box-like structure, directly on a wide sandy beach, just like Maria said. I ran down to the beach as soon as I got out of the car. The waves were lapping at the shore. Sea gulls were screaming and swooping down to the water to find their catch. Their flight, their silent gliding, so effortless, seemed so simple. Why does man have to be so complicated, needing machines, machines of destruction, to destroy each other. Why can't we just soar so effortlessly, so neatly, with just our bodies? Why do we need all this stuff, all these things that clutter our lives?

The air smelled clean. It was so pristine, so simple here, just the reeds, the dunes piled here and there, the lone seagull dipping in and out of the water. Yes, I could spend a month here. The cool breezes were blowing in off the Sound, in contrast to the suffocating heat in Manhattan. It was stifling there and I was starting to feel all closed in. Yes, it was good to be out of the city.

Sybil's house was ultra-modern, with a wall of thick opaque glass cubes separating the long living room from the dining room. Double green metal staircases spiraled up to the second floor and crossed mid-stream. Huge modern oil paintings covered the walls. The freedom of those splashes of reds and greens with wild swirls of colors was exhilarating to look at.

As Michael climbed the stairway to the second floor he thought, when I pick 'em, I sure pick 'em, or rather now as I remember it, she picked me.   As he was unpacking his clothes and hanging them up in the closet, he thought he should take Alan's advice and try, as he said, to not put all his eggs in one basket. But he was getting more and more emotionally entangled with Sybil and her crazy ways.

But Alan can help me, he thought, help me make some other connections. He said there were going to be people there at his party tomorrow night, people I should meet, producers and directors. He hinted he could help me with my career. Maybe he could help Melody too. I had to admit I had a soft spot for her. She was so sweet and innocent, naive really, for someone who grew up so close to New York, Queens, I think. Her parents must have really protected her.

Maria and Cecil had their own rooms here, just like in the apartment in Manhattan, but in a different wing of the house.

I was given a room right down the hallway from Sybil's. The first thing I tried to do was lock the door. Well, well, I must be moving up. This bedroom has a lock on the inside instead of the outside and had a pleasant summery feel to it. There was a big white shag rug spread out on the dark polished wood floor, and a large double window overlooking a garden. It had its own bathroom and came equipped with all the same men's toiletries as were in New York. From the second floor landing you could look out onto the two-storied living room's wall of glass to the blue Atlantic stretching off into the distance. It was truly spectacular.

As soon as I finished hanging up my clothes, I walked into Sybil's room as she was changing from her stiff grey New York suit to a relaxed blue and white striped shirt and capri pants. She turned to look at me in astonishment as if I had done the unthinkable.

"Michael, never, never do that again, walk in on me like that."

I didn't even answer her, I just walked up to her and grabbed her and kissed her in a way to show my love and appreciation for her. I didn't know if it was the ocean air, the freedom I felt out here, but I had to have her, I had to have her right then. And she looked truly beautiful, so different out here, sort of relaxed, as relaxed as I guess Sybil ever gets. I tried to move her over to the bed, but she pushed me away.

"No, Michael, not right now. We have something else I want us to do. Let's go down to the beach."

It was now dusk and the stars were starting to appear in the sky. We walked down the wooden stairway and through the torch-lit pathway down to the beach. The tall pampas grass was swaying in the breeze blowing in off the ocean and it reminded me of Sybil's hair, now long and loose, flowing and sensuous. It made me want to rip her clothes off right then and there and make mad love to her, right on the beach.

"The stars are especially bright tonight, aren't they." I took her hand and turned her toward me. I tried to kiss her again, and this time she let me, and it was a long passionate embrace.

"Michael, I have something special I want you to try."

"What is it, Sybil, what do you want me to try?"

"Magic mushrooms."

"Do you mean peyote?"

"Yes."

"Magic mushrooms, I heard of them. The Indians take them, don't they, for their rituals, their religion. They give the person taking them special powers, don't they."

"Yes, they're supposed to expand your consciousness. They say it will reveal what animal you are spiritually linked to. What animal are you, Michael??

"I don't know."

"Would you like to find out?"

"I don't know. I'm not sure. I've never tried it before."

We sat down next to a dune and I looked out at the moon lit ocean. It was so peaceful. The moonlight was illuminating the gentle little waves lapping at the shore. All I could think of was making love to Sybil, right here, right now on the beach. But when I tried to put my arm around her and draw here closer to me, she just pushed me away.

"Here, try these."

Michael took the handful of shriveled up mushrooms and swallowed them. Then they walked hand in hand toward the surf. He felt the cold waves brush up against his bare feet. Soon the clouds seemed to be moving faster and faster, swirling round and round, and they started to assume strange shapes. The stars were getting brighter and brighter and the moon was so gigantic it looked like it was about to engulf the entire earth. The clouds were forming into the most fantastic shapes, animal shapes. Lizards and dragons and giant sea serpents were rising up out of the ocean. They all seemed so gentle though, not the roaring fire-breathing kind. They were all looking for something, sniffing at the air. What were they looking for? Then I heard her voice, like from a great distance, even though I knew she was standing right next to me. Sybil was calling my name, "Michael, Michael, are you all right?" It was all muffled. I could hardly hear her.

And then the most incredible thing happened. Sybil was no longer standing next to me, but she had transformed herself into a giant hawk and then she took flight, circling above me with great outstretched brown wings and giant claws hanging down. Then with no warning, she suddenly came swooping down in a terrifying way and clutched me by her long talons. She picked me up and carried me aloft, like I was just its small prey. We climbed to an incredible height. We soared above the ocean and glided over the waves glimmering in the moonlight. I could see the whole ocean, all the way down the coastline, stretching on for miles and miles, the white lace brushing the shore. I could even see the curve of the ocean, falling off into the distance. And the stars, the stars were so close and intense, I thought we were going to fly right into one. Then suddenly I felt like I was going to be dropped, dropped from that great height and smashed down back onto the beach. But no, she was now gliding, gliding down gently, holding me still, until we were almost there, and then she let go. I fell a short drop to the warm sandy beach. As I sprawled out on the sand, it felt good to be back down. I started to crawl and sniff the ground. Then I felt my whiskers move, to shake out a few grains of sand. I was a mouse, a common ordinary field mouse. I twitched my whiskers again and felt the fur stand up down the middle of my back. Danger, danger, watch out! Danger close by. Then I saw it, it was closing in on me, sneaking up, hunched down, its back arched, its huge yellow eyes gleaming in the dark. The frightening cold heartless black slits were just staring at me, like I was an object. And it was coming right at me. It was the most gigantic ferocious cat I'd ever seen, a monster. I tried to run, but suddenly I found myself paralyzed with fear and couldn't move. My feet were glued to the sand.

There was nothing I could do. In a moment, the cat was upon me.

It started scratching, clawing, tearing at my flesh. I had to escape, but I couldn't move. I was caught in its grasp and it wouldn't release me. The more I struggled, the deeper it tore into my flesh with its claws. I knew I'd have to be very still if I was going to survive. Maybe it would get tired of its game and just go away. But no, it held firm. Then I blacked out.

CHAPTER 9 - Saturday, August 2, East Hampton

When I finally woke up the next morning. It was dawn and I was back in my room, upstairs at Sybil's house at the beach. I had no idea how I got there. At least the visions of last night didn't seem real anymore. It was the peyote and I vowed I would never take it again.

Playing on the floor with a catnip mouse was a large orange stripped tabby cat, meowing and rolling around on the white rug in a patch of sunlight. I got up, stumbled around the cat, and made my groggy way into the bathroom. I splashed cold water on my face. Then I turned and looked in the mirror. Then I saw it, tiny scratches all over my shoulders and back.

What about the visions of last night on the beach, obviously induced by the peyote. I'd heard about it before, but never tried it, and never experienced anything like it. Boy, I could teach

Harry something about getting into the psyche of an animal back in acting class. But now, to my chagrin, I remembered, to my horror and pain, I'd been a lowly mouse, passive and defenseless. Was that really me? Was that really what I was supposed to be, all rot, all mush, and no will power, no resistance?

"NO," I shouted out loud, "NO." I had to change that. That just couldn't be it. I couldn't allow that to be me. There had to be more to me than that.

Sybil had said something about going shopping today in East Hampton. I'd make some excuse, sneak off and phone Melody and make sure she was coming to Alan's party tonight. I had to see her. She did say she'd go, that she'd be there. But maybe after I didn't show up for the producer's reading, she wouldn't come. I had to call her to make absolutely sure. That's it, I'd offer to meet her at the train station and then we could go the party together. The two of us would get Alan to introduce us to those powerful film people who were going to be there.

The door to my room opened. It was Maria, the maid.

"Don't tell her I spoke to you. Madame doesn't like me to speak to the guests, but you better get dressed. Madame is taking you to town for lunch . . . and shopping," she said with a smile on her face.

An open red Jeep was backing out of the garage as I stepped out of house into the bright sunlight. I had expected Cecil to be in the driver's seat, but it was Sybil, looking very attractive in a Hermes silk scarf wrapped around her dark hair, wearing big dark sunglasses. She had on a red silk pants suit that seemed to match her jeep, and she looked delicious.

"C'mon, big guy, we're off."

I was barely able to hop in over the door as she started to take off down the driveway, and then she sped at a dangerous and frightening speed down the winding lane, screeching the tires and almost two wheeling it onto the main road.

As we were walking into the Ralph Lauren store in the village, Sybil ran into two friends of hers. They had their kids in tow.

"Sybil, we didn't know you were out here yet. We heard you were filming in New York. We were just talking about you the other day. We were wondering when you were going to settle down, you know, find a nice husband." They both looked Michael up and down with disapproval.

"Well, you two dears can just keep wondering. I never want to find a 'nice' husband and I never want to 'settle down.' I never want a man in my house telling me what to do. Now does that answer your question, ladies."

"But Sybil, we're only trying help. And frankly, we're worried about you. You know you're not getting any younger. Aren't you ever going to get married?

"Please don't worry yourselves about me. The idea of a husband dates back to the middle ages, when a wife was the property of her husband. I prefer to own my own property, thank you."

And with that, Sybil turned on her heels and walked us right into the store.

"Sybil, that was rude, the way you left them."

"I think they were rude. Why don't they mind their own damn business and just go on leading their dull little lives. But no, they want to mind everyone else's business. Why do they think everyone has to fit into the same little shoe that they picked out at the same little store."

"I guess you're right."

"Of course, I'm right. Now let's pick out some nice summer outfits for you. I think this one will look great. And this one, and how about this one. It'll go great with this woven belt and these boating shoes. I just love this blue seersucker suit and this blue cashmere sweater."

The Ralph Lauren clothes were piled high in my arms. It looked like she was buying up half the store. "You're not expecting me to try all this on, are you? I'll take half the afternoon."

"Of course not. You can try them on at home."

Michael laid down all the clothes on the counter for the sales girl to ring up.

"Here miss," Sybil handed the girl her charge card.

"That'll be nine hundred seventy-five dollars. Sign here."

"Now that's all taken care of, let's go to lunch. I'm famished, aren't you?

"I'm ready to eat a horseburger. I mean a burger as big as a horse."

Michael piled all the bags into the back seat of the jeep and they drove a short way to Hampton Point. The inside of the restaurant had a slick Manhattan look, white linen table cloths and walls of glass with a magnificent view of the yachts bobbing about in the grey choppy waters of Long Island Sound. Inside next to the bar was a real thirty foot sloop, sails and all, soaring up to the second floor ceiling. The long bar was all polished wood and brass. There was a large deck right at the water's edge and a locked gated walkway to the yachts. The place was packed with the Saturday lunch crowd. The maitre'd seemed to know

Sybil and gave us a table right away that had a wonderful view of the harbor. Sybil ordered cold poached salmon with dill sauce and a flute of champagne. I ordered two cheeseburgers with fries and a Heineken. The waiter brought out two little tiny cups filled with ketchup. You could never get enough ketchup in a place like that.

"Look, its Alan and Eric with Annize and her new boyfriend Don. She would have taken a liking to you, but I think I talked her out of it. I convinced her it wouldn't be healthy for her career. I didn't know I would start getting attached to you like this. You know it's funny. You never know who you're going to like, sometimes it's the most unlikely people, the person you'd never think it's going to be in a million years."

"What do you mean, not in a million years? I don't know whether to take that as a compliment or an insult. What are they all doing out here, anyways?" I was trying to act as if I didn't know about the party, to see her reaction.

"Alan has a great house, not far from mine, not on the beach, mind you, but a big old fussy affair, one of those big gloomy shingled jobs that stretch on forever with big rolling lawns. And Annize rented a small cape in Water Mill. Didn't I tell you, we're resuming filming here on Monday? A lot of location shooting. Alan is concerned. I've got a lot of preparation to do, last minute things to make sure everything goes smoothly."

The waiter brought out the poached salmon and Michael's burger and fries. A sommelier brought out the beer and champagne on a tray. Michael immediately took a bite of the thick burger and then dipped his French fries into the tiny cup of ketchup.

"So tonight, it's early to bed, early to rise. Tomorrow morning I've planned a ride for us on the beach at Montauk, just the two of us."

"Sybil, I'd like to find a nice deserted cove among the dunes, pull you off your horse and make love to you for hours and hours, and then walk along the sand hand in hand and let the surf lap at our feet."

"Michael, I didn't know you were so romantic." She took a sip of her champagne.

"I'm not really. It's you Sybil, you're bringing it out in me. Excuse me for a moment. I'll be right back."

Michael hurried to find the men's room and a phone. He quickly dialed Melody's number.

"Hello, Melody?"

"Michael, where are you? Where the hell were you yesterday? Our big scene, remember, in front of the producers. I was counting on you and you let me down in a big way. I shouldn't even be talking to you now. I should hang up the phone."

"Melody, I'm sorry. Don't hang up."

"This better be good."

"I really wanted to be there, believe me. I wanted to be there really bad. So bad I could taste it. But I couldn't. I just couldn't go."

"Oh, yeah, and why not? The big chance we were both waiting for, the reading we prepared so hard for. You lost us the chance to be on Broadway and start our careers."

"Off Broadway, remember."

"So what. Off Broadway, Off Off Broadway, who cares. That's where a lot of actors get their start. "

"Name one that I ever heard of."

"How about Dustin Hoffman. That's where Mike Nichols spotted him before casting him in the 'Graduate'."

"Well, there'll be other readings, I'm sure."

"You make so light of it."

"Melody, I can't talk right now. I want you to take the train out. I'll meet you at the station at nine tonight. I'm already out here in South Hampton. We'll go to Alan's party together."

"Well, I don't know. Your track record so far is not too good."

"Melody, I promise I'll be there. Please tell me you'll come."

"Well, I don't know."

"Say yes, besides you already told Alan you'd be there. There's going to be lots of film people there."

"Well, O.K. I guess you talked me into it."

"Great, I'll be there at nine sharp, and I really want to see you again."

"O.K. Michael, you're a great talker. I'll see you tonight at nine. You better be there and be on time."

I felt great as I sprinted back to the table. Sybil was settling up with the waiter and Alan was sitting in my chair chatting with her. "

"Anyways Sybil, I know you'll be bored with all the stiffs I'm having over. You never liked mingling with the, as you say, the fake east coast crowd."

"No, I won't be there. Michael and I are going to spend a quiet evening at home. We have an early morning planned for Sunday, horseback riding on the beach."

"Oh, Michael. How's it going? Enjoying our glorious weather?" Alan noticed me standing there as he got up from my seat.

"Yes, it's been great."

"Planning to be out here for awhile, I hope."

Sybil interrupted me before I could speak, "Well, we have to get going Alan."

"See you during the week for lunch, perhaps? Alan asked.

"How about Monday? There's a new project I'm planning for my next film, and I want to talk to you about it. The screenplay's shaping up great. I think you're going to like it."

Sybil got up to leave.

"That's perfect. Just call me Sunday night to confirm. I better get back to my guests." Alan walked back to his table.

Michael thought that was close. I thought she was going to accept Alan's invitation to his party. Now all I have to do is figure out how to get out of the house and back in without being noticed later tonight.

Annize walked up to Sybil just as we were leaving. "Sybil, I'm a total wreck. Can I come over Sunday to go over my scenes. I don't know if I can handle it. I think I'm having a nervous breakdown. The scenes are so emotional."

"I guess I better spare you a few minutes. How about four o'clock? This film's my most important project to date. My career sinks or swims on this one, so you better not let me down Annize. I know you can do it."

"That's right Sybil, keep telling me stuff like that."

"Better make it five."

Alan came over to join Annize. "Sybil, I guess you know how critical this film is to your career. Your last two weren't that well received and well, the studio is getting nervous. They're concerned about all this location shooting, and they might send their watchdogs down."

"Alan, please keep them away, that's all I need."

"O.K. Sybil, I'll see what I can do. But if it looks like you're running over and we get close to having those performance bond assholes coming down on us, we're going to have to send our own people in to take over the picture."

"Thanks a lot Alan. That's all I need. I know I can count on you to keep them away."

"Sybil, if you do have a hit with this one, your career could skyrocket and I could possibly get you a multi-picture development deal. On the other hand, if you fuck up..."

"Thanks Alan, you're so encouraging."

"I'm the one who pushed this one at the final meeting, so it's my neck on the line too."

"Let's talk again Sunday night, Alan."

When we returned to Sybil's glass house, I went for a swim in the ocean and worked on my tan. Sybil was busy in her study preparing for the week's shoot. It seemed like just an ordinary Saturday afternoon out in the Hamptons.

CHAPTER 10 - Saturday, August 2, East Hampton

That evening, Cecil lit a fire in the study. She looked different tonight. She had on a frilly shirt and black velvet pants. I'd never seen her out of her chauffeur's uniform. She always seemed so cold and official. I'd never really given her much thought, except as Sybil's policeman and driver. I wasn't sure I liked the way she was looking at Sybil. It was a little too friendly, a little too warm. In a way, I felt left out and I didn't like it. Sybil was going over some paperwork in a big easy chair at her desk.

There was a cool breeze billowing in through the heavy damask drapery. The sweet scent of the wildflowers was so strong it was intoxicating. I stood by the window, listening to the surf pounding on the beach. It had a soothing sound, like a mother rocking a baby in her arms. Sybil looked at me over her reading glasses. She looked more serious than usual, more intellectual and impressive with her glasses on.

"Michael, put on that Billy Holiday C.D. for me. It's in the cabinet to the right."

"Ain't Nobody's Business" started playing and it certainly fit Sybil.

"There ain't nothing I can do or nothing I can say that folks don't criticize me, but I'm going to do just as I want to anyway. I don't care what people say . . . If my man ain't got no money and I said take all of mine, honey, ain't nobody's business if I do.."

I still had to figure out how to get out of there. How the hell was I going to do that? Sybil got up and poured some port out of a decanter. I encouraged her to drink more as we toasted each other. She went back to sit at her desk. I kissed her on the back of her neck as I stood behind her and gently massaged her shoulders. The heat from the fire and the dark red wine were making me drowsy and I hoped it was making Sybil tired too.

I tried to kiss her on her lips and suggested we go to her

bedroom, but she pushed me away and laughed, "No, not now Michael, I have more work to do. I can hardly keep eyes open. The ocean air always makes me so tired at night. I think I'm going to retire early, by myself, and catch up on my sleep."

"You don't mind then, Sybil? I'm kind of tired myself after last night. I could use a solid night's sleep after all that shopping. I haven't even tried on all those Ralph Lauren clothes you bought me today."

"That's a good idea, why don't you go and see if they fit."

"I really don't need all that stuff."

"Yes you do, if you're going to be seen around here with me."

Michael planted a long passionate kiss, forcing her to stand so he could embrace her.

"Goodnight Sybil, I think I'm falling in love with you."

"Silly boy. Good night."

Michael graciously backed out of the paneled study, bowing and scraping, making believe he was waving a large brimmed hat with long ostrich plumes, sweeping the floor, back and forth, like a musketeer for his lady.

Michael hurried to his room and locked the door. He had to think fast. This was great. What a break about Sybil working late and wanting to retire by herself. It was still risky business, but he had to do it. It was already eight o'clock. It was still early but he had to be careful. He couldn't make one noise. He couldn't let anyone know he was leaving the house. He looked out the window of his room. There was a ledge and a gutter. It looked pretty solid. The rain gutter was next to a big old oak tree. Even better. He stuffed some towels and linens under the covers to make it look like he was asleep in his bed in case anyone looked in. He shut off all the lights.

In the moonlight illuminating the room, he took one last look around, and then went out the window. Holding onto the gutter, he climbed over onto the tree. It brought back memories of his childhood at the farm when he put a few boards up in an old apple tree and called it his tree house. That was the only place he ever really felt at home when he lived with his aunt and uncle.

He looked out at the ocean and thought how far he had come from all that. He got close to the ground and then jumped down the rest of the way. He ran through the thick stand of white birch trees to the winding road, staying close the trees so he would not be seen from the house. When he got to the road, he put out his thumb and began trying to hitch a ride. Soon a rusty old green pick-up truck stopped.

The old man asked, "Where ya' going?"

"The train station in town."

"Sure hop in. I'm going into town myself, to throw down a few cold ones. Don't want to join me, do you? Got to get away from the missus for a few hours now and then. Know what I mean?"

If only I had told him I had changed my mind, that I didn't need a ride after all and headed back to the house, back to my room, back to Sybil, then none of this would have happened. If only I hadn't taken that ride to the train station to pick up Melody and taken her to Alan's house. When you're somewhere you're not supposed to be, doing something you're not supposed to be doing, with someone you're not supposed to be doing it with, that's when all the trouble begins. But instead, I got into the old man's truck.

"So, you want to join me?"

"Sorry, I'd like to have a drink with you, maybe another time, but I got to pick someone up at the train station, someone coming in from New York, and I promised to be there at nine."

"Yeah, sure, no problem. I'll get you there by nine. You got plenty of time," the man said as he checked his watch, causing him to swerve, barely missing an oncoming truck that blasted its horn three times.

"Thanks, thanks alot, but I'm really not in that much of a hurry."

"Yeah, you're right, that was a close call."

The man let Michael out in front of the station at exactly five minutes before nine. He started to breathe a little easier now. He rushed up to the platform and heard the sharp blast of the whistle as the train pulled into the station. He could hardly wait to hold her in his arms. Maybe he would start to understand what was happening to him, it was all so confusing. Finally the train pulled up to the platform, its brakes screeching loudly.

A few people got off, but there was no sign of Melody. Where the hell was she? Did she even get on that train? Maybe she changed her mind and hadn't forgiven me. But then there she was, stepping out of the train, a vision in white, in a white tulle dress with a white scarf floating around her neck, and white satin pumps. She was carrying a small black overnight case.

"Melody over here."

She rushed over to me. "Michael, you're here, and on time. I was afraid you wouldn't show up as usual and I'd have to go to Alan's party by myself."

CHAPTER 11 - Tuesday, August 5
Riverhead Correctional Facility

I almost forgot, when I woke up it was morning and I was still in jail. Trying to sleep in that cell was no laughing matter. Herman, my cell mate, was a black man in his forties. He told me he was in for armed robbery. I asked him why he did it.

"Hey, I'm a family man with four kids. I was desperate. I needed the money. I wasn't thinking straight, and now this."

"They say they got a confession out of me after I was arrested and interrogated for hours. I don't remember confessing to any murder, but it's all a blur now. I know I'm being framed for it. I was there. I saw it happen, but I swear I didn't do it," Michael explained to Herman.

I started telling him about Saturday night when we were interrupted by a guard announcing "Visitor for Michael Connell." I had used my one call to Sybil, but her maid Maria had answered and said "Madame is out on location and won't be available until

149

later this evening." I pleaded with her to try to get ahold of her, explaining my situation and where I was. Maybe it was Sybil, coming through for me at last.

The guard put handcuffs on me and led me down the walkway to a small room. A fat man in his late thirties, with thick black rimmed glasses, wearing a cheap creased grey suit came waddling into the room. He was carrying a scuffed up brown leather briefcase.

"My name is Kapp, Attorney John Kapp."

"So Sybil got my message and is going to help me out after all."

"No, I'm afraid not. You see I'm the public defender assigned to your case. I've been appointed by the court to represent you."

"What?"

"Yes, unless you want to pay for someone else and hire your own attorney. But from what I was told, you don't have the funds to do so."

"No, you're right, I don't have any funds. But Sybil, I think she's going to hire a lawyer for me. Has anyone called the court yet?"

"Nobody's called, that I'm aware of."

"No one? Are you sure?"

"I'm afraid so. That's why I've been appointed to represent you, and you have a hearing coming up in two days, your arraignment.

"Swell, that's great. I guess you better go ahead."

"I'll do the best I can for you. Those are serious charges, very serious. They could send you away for life if you're found guilty."

"Life?"

"Yes, I'm afraid so. Actually two life sentences. One for each murder. That's the worse you can get in this state. New York doesn't have the death penalty."

"Great, now they're charging me with a second murder?"

"Yes, that's right, that happened on the same night, a female.

So why don't you just cooperate with me and tell me the truth and I'll see what I can do for you."

"I've been telling the truth. I'm innocent."

"I know, but the report I read of your statement after your arrest sounds like you made a confession. About killing the guy."

"I didn't do it!"

"It says right here in the transcript that you admitted it. You said you used a knife."

"I didn't do it, I didn't confess to anything. They twisted my words around. They got me confused after hours of questioning. I didn't have a lawyer there with me."

"They say you waved your Miranda rights. Look, we're wasting time. Why don't you just tell me your version. Start from the beginning with last Saturday night. Try not to leave anything out. It's that little detail that just might save your neck. Then I'll worry what to do about the confession."

"O.K., I'll try to remember."

He had a tape recorder going and also took notes. Maybe he

would be all right after all. He seemed pretty serious about defending me. Besides, I didn't have much choice. He'd better be damn good, especially with that confession.

I started to tell him how I met Melody at the train station on that Saturday night.

CHAPTER 12 - Saturday Evening, August 2

East Hampton

"Melody was a beautiful girl, only seventeen, that I met at the acting school in Manhattan. We were taking classes together. I promised I'd meet her at the train station in East Hampton at nine. We'd been invited to a party given by Alan. He said there were going to be producers and directors there that could help our acting careers. I got to the station right on time and there she was, stepping off the train, a vision in white, in a white tulle dress, a white scarf floating from her neck, and little white satin pumps. She was carrying a small black overnight case. She didn't see me, so I yelled to her, "Melody over here."

She rushed over to me. "Michael, you're here, and on time. I was afraid you wouldn't show up, as usual and I'd have to go to Alan's party by myself."

"No Melody, I'm right here, in the flesh."

I gave her a warm welcome, held her in my arms and gave her a long deep kiss. I didn't realize my feelings for her had grown so much. We climbed down the stairs to the street and I hailed a cab. Melody looked at the card Alan had given her at the Met and told the driver Alan's address.

As soon as they got in the cab, Michael tried to kiss her again. He put one hand down the front of her low cut dress and the other up her skirt all the way to her lacy underwear, but she used all her strength to push him away.

"No Michael, not here."

"Then she started, "You could have at least called me to let me know you weren't coming to the reading the other morning. You made a fool of me. I kept looking at the door of the class all morning, expecting to see you walk in at any moment, late as usual. But no, Michael, nothing."

"Please, Melody, I told you I couldn't make it. And I didn't have time to call you. I had to leave right away, unexpectedly, to come out here."

"Michael, I don't understand why you let both of us down. It was our big chance. Can't you at least explain why you didn't come to the reading? You owe me that much."

"I told you Melody I had to be out here. That's all there is to it."

"I think at least you would have gotten chosen for the part. Probably not me, but you, they would have chosen you. And you threw your chance away, just like that?"

"Hey, I don't think I'm that good. They probably would have chosen some one else anyways."

"Michael, why do you sell yourself so short? You were great in that scene and everyone said so. I could see the teacher was impressed, even if he didn't come right out and say so. And if the teacher is impressed at the Stasberg Institute, it really means something."

"Let's just drop it, O.K. and start enjoying the evening," he said, putting his arms around her. "There'll be other chances, maybe even tonight."

She pushed him away, "No, Michael, not now."

"I thought we were supposed to be together this evening, having a good time. That's what you came out here for, wasn't it, or are you just going to spend the whole evening telling me off."

Soon the driver was pulling up the long driveway to Alan's house. He stopped in front of an impressive looking rambling grey shingled mansion, even much grander than Sybil had described it. He paid the cab driver, who then pulled away around the circular driveway

Michael was standing there, looking up at the house. He had a funny feeling of foreboding, a strange misgiving and he felt he should have never left Sybil's house, and he felt especially that he should have never brought Melody here. But she was his protection. No, nothing was going to happen to him tonight. He wouldn't let his guard down for a minute. He could hear music coming from the back of the house, some old jazz tunes. There were lots of cars parked out front, about thirty or more. There were Rolls Royces, Mercedes, a Ferrari here and there, and a few Jeeps, Jags and Porsches.

They walked in the front door of the magnificent house. A huge crystal chandelier hung down over the foyer. There were oriental rugs with the patina of age on vast expanses of dark polished wood floors. A butler in uniform guided them out to the manicured grounds in the back of the house where the party was in full swing. There was an enormous swimming pool that looked like a natural rock grotto. Three fully clothes guests, two guys and a girl, were pushed into the pool and they started splashing around. A stunning girl with long blond hair took off her dress to reveal a g-string bikini and then dove in. Two guys stripped down to their briefs and jumped in right after her.

I spotted Annize over by the bar with her boyfriend Don. He was young, blond and tanned. She looked wonderful in her halter top, love beads and bell bottom pants, her long dark hair cascading down her back. It was all very festive with the brightly colored Japanese lanterns strung everywhere. Torches lit the pathways which were dotted with topiary figures. There was a jazz trio playing music from the thirties by Cole Porter. A male singer in a tuxedo was singing, 'I get a kick from champagne, pure alcohol doesn't thrill me at all, so tell me why should it be true, that I get a kick out of you. Some get a kick from cocaine ...'

I led Melody over to the bar to get us some drinks. Annize led Don away as we were approaching, and started introducing him to everyone. He looked awkward and looked like he wished he was anywhere but there. Don led Annize back to the bar. Guess he needed another drink.

"Michael, you naughty boy. If you're very very good, I won't tell Sybil. We'll keep your little secret. Only kidding, sort of."

Michael shot her a dirty look.

"Whoops, always putting my foot in it. Who's your little friend? Of course, I can blackmail you, you know."

He had to get her away from Melody. "Excuse us for a moment, I'll be right back."

Michael firmly took Annize by the arm and led her away from the bar. "Annize, are you crazy?"

"I won't tell Sybil your little secret. It'll be hush hush just between us, but believe me she won't like it, she won't like it one little bit. If she were ever to find out you came to this party with some young thing . . . So buddy boy, I think you're going to owe me one. You've got to get me a copy of her new script, the one she keeps talking about doing next."

"Annize, you know that's impossible. She'll know I took it if she finds it gone."

"Well, go ahead and introduce me to your pretty little friend." She took my hand and led us back to the bar.

Melody and Don were talking to each other and sipping their champagne.

"Annize, this is Melody. We met at acting school and Alan invited her to this party."

"Nice to meet you. Annize? Oh, Annize! I just loved your last album. I bought it and played it over and over again."

"Why thanks, thank you very much. Michael, I'm beginning to like your new friend. Did I tell you she has terrific taste, especially in music," she laughed as she took a sip of her champagne.

"Thanks Annize, glad you approve. Where's Alan? I haven't seen him yet."

"Oh, he's around, somewhere, mingling with all his guests."

"Yeah, there he is, probably making some new deals. Playing every moment for all its worth."

"Great place he has here."

"Yeah, and he has one in Paris, one on the west coast, and one in London. Oh, Alan's quite a mover and shaker."

"We know. We met him in New York," Melody added.

"If I were you, I'd listen to what he says. He's very smart. He's helped my career alot. Look what he's doing for Sybil. He's the one that got her financing for her latest film."

"By the way, why didn't you tell me about Sybil? Who is she?"

"She's a film producer, that's all."

"Oh, I see. That's not the way Annize made it sound."

"Melody, let's not get into that right now. Can't we just enjoy ourselves and not get into another argument?"

"O.K. Michael, have it your way."

"That's better." Michael kissed her in the same way that set them off in that empty classroom back at the Institute. He waltzed her over to behind a grove of thick trees so they couldn't be seen from the pool area by any of the guests. He almost ripped the buttons off his shirt, he had to have her right then and there. He was tearing her clothes off and made mad passionate love to her under the stars, just like their first time together in that empty classroom. He knew she wanted him, even though she tried to resist at first. The musicians were playing, "You're the top, you're the coliseum, you're the top, you're a new museum, you're a melody in a symphony, you're a Shakespeare sonnet, you're a trip down the Nile, you're the Tower of Pisa, you're the smile of the Mona Lisa, I'm a worthless chap, if I'm the bottom, you're the top."

The stars had come out quite brightly in the night sky, and Michael felt happy as he looked up and felt part of the strange swirling universe out there. But then it came back to him, and he couldn't get Annize's comments out of his mind. They both rearranged their clothes so they could rejoin the guests.

"Melody, I can't keep it to myself any longer. I have to tell you something. I hope you won't be mad at me."

"Michael, what is it?"

"I slept with Annize once, it was nothing and it was before I met you." She doesn't mean anything to me. She was O.K. for a one night stand, but she wanted it to continue it and I didn't." I think I knew what she meant by her blackmail scheme and I didn't like it one bit.

"So that's why she said those things."

"Yes."

"Michael, I'm worried about you."

"What? What are you worried about?"

"Don't you know?" You don't seem in control and you always seem so distracted all the time. You don't make any sense. You're not focused. Why are you doing this to yourself?"

"Stop it Melody. I know what I'm doing and I'm doing what I want."

"That's what you think, Michael."

They spotted Alan winding his way through the crowd toward them.

"Alan, we've been looking all over for you and wondering if the host forgot to show up at his own party."

As Alan sipped his cocktail, he eyed Michael carefully. "Are you two enjoying yourselves. I'm glad you both decided to come. Quite festive here tonight, isn't it."

Eric came over to join Alan. Eric was a blond boy, about twenty who Michael had seen with Alan at the costume ball in New York and at lunch at the Yacht Club. Eric put his arm around Alan's shoulders. Eric looked drunk.

Then I noticed the tall blond woman and the older man were there too, the same ones who were at the bar the night I met Sybil. I didn't know why, but it was making me nervous. Several of the guests were coming over to thank Alan for the wonderful evening. They were leaving. It was almost midnight.

"Alan, I think we should be leaving too."

"No stay, the party's really just getting started."

Melody would have to chime in, "Alan's right. We only got here just a little while ago."

"You should listen to her more often. And she looks so pretty tonight." I didn't like the way Alan took her hand in his. Melody knew Alan was a big cheese with one of the studios. It made me wonder if that's why she came all the way out here tonight, not just to see me. Now that she was talking to Alan, there was no way of getting her out of there. And what if Sybil went to my room to check on me. I had to get back to the house and I just had to get Melody on that last train back to New York.

Melody cheerfully announced, "Guess what, Michael, Alan wants me to stay over so I don't have to take that late train back tonight."

"Oh, great."

"I have a beautiful guest room just waiting for you overlooking the ocean." Alan looked at his Patek Philippe watch, "And you're probably going to miss that train anyways."

"Really, Melody, we have to go.

"And let that guest room go to waste. You could use the beach in the morning and go for a nice swim and go back after lunch."

I tried my best to get her to leave, but I was no match for Alan.

"C'mon Melody, we really should leave. You can still make that train if we hurry"

I took her arm and tried to start walking her out, but she pulled away from me.

"No, Michael, I'm staying."

I could see there was no budging her, "O.K., have it your way."

Damn it, now I would have to stay there with her until she went to her room. Hopefully, Sybil had gone to bed by now.

But I really wanted to get back to Sybil. Whenever I was away from her for too long, it was like a magnet started to pull me back to her, so powerful was the attraction. It was the chemistry, it was the fantasy. It was incredible now that I thought about it. Whenever I touched Sybil, I just started to burn up, the contact was so fiery. And Melody was just being stupid, naive really, taken in by Alan. I had to get her to leave.

"Melody, we really should leave, right now."

"You can leave if you want to, but I'm staying."

"Hey you two, come on downstairs. The fun is just beginning, now that the booring set has left."

There were a few people still there, but most had already left.

"There's a group downstairs already watching some movies in my screening room. And there'll be a champagne buffet right afterwards."

The jazz trio was playing, "What is This Thing Called Love."

I could see there was no talking Melody out of it as Alan led us down a spiral set of stairs. "In my youth, a long time ago. I remember it so well, I saw Marlon, the great Marlon Brando in the first stage production of the play, appearing as Stanley Kowalski on opening night. What a magnificent animal he was, and he was so perfect for the part, electrifying really."

Alan was leading us down a long corridor. It looked just like an art gallery with both sides lined with huge black paintings. Nothing but huge blotches of black paint on unprimed white canvases. They were all signed, "Rothko."

"I wish I could have seen him perform," Melody sighed.

"And you should have seen Tennessee backstage that night, all nerves. He was pacing back and forth and twisting the ends of his moustache until I thought they would fall off. And it's funny, no matter how brilliant they are, they never really know their own genius until someone else appreciates it for them. They are the most insecure human beings on the face of the earth. And contradictory too. Writers are the most egotistical people you'll ever want to meet. How else could they put their pitiful little lives on paper and think it would be interesting enough to entertain you and me? But somehow they do it. Self doubt, the poisonous eater of men's souls. It will cripple you, if you let it."

"Did Michael tell you how he blew the Broadway producer reading by not showing up?"

"Michael, if you don't have confidence in yourself, no one else will either," Alan offered.

"That wasn't it, that wasn't it at all."

"Of course, it takes time to polish your craft. It doesn't just come overnight. Great actors aren't born, they develop."

"Then there's hope," Melody added.

Alan noticed me looking at the paintings. "Do you like them? They're by Mark Rothko. This series was done right before he committed suicide, and he was a successful artist too. What a pity."

"Michael, I think you have a great future ahead of you, after hearing you read at "21," and I don't want to see you waste it."

I know Alan was referring to Sybil. Alan pushed open a grey suede door and we entered a small screening room. It had grey suede walls and red plush theatre seats. There were a few people seated watching a film flickering in the darkness.

We all sat down in the last row before I realized what was on the screen. It was pornography. There were naked men and naked women on the screen and they were crawling around on the floor. One of the men, a primitive looking type, crawled up behind one of the women and mounted her from behind, thrusting into her. The man looked like he was enjoying himself, but the woman looked uncomfortable. Actually, there was a look of pain on her face, not physical pain, but extreme mental anguish. I had to get Melody out of there.

"Alan, I think we better go."

Melody was in shock, with a strange blank look on her face.

"No, Michael, you don't like this sort of entertainment, do you? Then come with me. We don't have to stay here watching this. Just come with me, there's some other people I'd like you to meet."

We got up and left the theatre room. Melody and I followed Alan down the hallway. Alan opened a door. We could see it was Eric, chained up facing the wall. His back was bloody. He had an iron collar around his neck. The older man, Alan's friend, was standing there with a whip in his hand. He watched us enter the room. The tall blond woman was there too. She was just standing there. Eric looked scared. I could tell he didn't want to be there.

"Michael, this is Eric," Alan said in the most casual of manners, which made it seem even more bizarre, as if he was introducing someone over tea at a country club. Melody had turned into a zombie-like state and no longer seemed to be reacting to anything.

"Michael, take off your jacket. Make yourself comfortable. This is what you chose. You came to me. You want me to do something for you, to help you, don't you? Well, let me tell you, first it's your turn to do something for me, and your pretty little friend too, that you so nicely escorted to my garden party."

"Alan, I think you're making a big mistake."

"No Michael, I'm not making a mistake. I think it's you and all those like you who always want something for nothing. You make no effort of your own, you just waltz in and try to waltz through life on someone else's back, on someone else's hard won efforts. On someone else's lifelong struggle, giving their blood, their sweat, even their tears. But they mean nothing to you, their struggles, their tears. No, you care nothing about them, because there is only yourself, your own dear selfish carcass. No, we're supposed to do all the sweating for you, and what do you do ingrate?"

Alan was yelling now, raving like a madman.

"You do g-ddamn nothing and expect the world to roll over for you. But I think you're going to roll over for me tonight, Michael, like you've never rolled over before."

Alan was screaming right in my face and I could smell his boozy breath. He was drunk. He tried to grab me, but I pushed him away and then with no warning, he punched me right in the face. I lost my balance and his friend, the older man, grabbed hold of me. I struggled with them as they grabbed my arms and pinned them behind me, twisting my arms as they both pushed me over to the wall, the wall right next to Eric. I kicked at them as I struggled, but the two men together were too much for me. I could not break loose from their grip.

"Melody, run, get out of here!" She tried the door, but it was locked. "Scream, bang on the door, someone will hear you."

She pounded on the door with her fists and screamed, "Someone, someone please, let me out of here! Please let us out!' She was hysterical and then she crumpled to the floor crying.

Alan continued ranting as he and his friend fastened handcuffs to my wrists, attaching one arm at a time to chains on the wall. "All you do is take, you eat, you're nothing but a human compost machine, you're worthless human garbage."

I managed to kick Alan good and hard in the stomach before the two men shackled my ankles to the wall too. Then Alan punched me hard on the mouth, making my lip bleed.

"Makes for nice red lipstick." Alan took his finger and spread the blood on my lips. I could taste the salt as I tried to lick it off with my tongue. Melody was crumpled up on the floor next to the door. Her crying was more muted now.

"Here, try some of this. It will make you feel better." He had calmed down now that I was helpless and chained to the wall. Now Alan was trying to act nice to me. He held some white powder up to my nose. "Go ahead, try it, you might like it."

"I don't want any of your drugs. I don't want any of that cocaine."

"Oh, it's not cocaine, its heroin. I don't think you and your friend are going to have any choice in what you're going to be doing for the rest of the night. So go ahead, and snort some. It's the finest, the finest that money can buy. That's all I ever have around me," he said as he looked over at Eric.

Alan held the white powder right under Michael's nose. He held his breath as long as he could, but finally he had to take a breath and it went right up his nasal passages.

"Ever had this stuff before? Nice pure heroin. Takes awhile to get used to it. Usually makes you sick the first time. But shortly everything will seem all right, then everything will be golden and nothing will seem to matter to you anymore. All those things that tortured you and bothered your brain and ripped at your heart, none of that will matter anymore."

"You have me, why don't you just let Melody go?" Michael pleaded with Alan.

"It all seems so insignificant and you wonder why you ever worried about any of it in the first place. Next, you'll wonder why you never saw things like this before. This seems like the reality. And then you'll never want to be in that other horrible superficial reality again. All it does is make you suffer." Then Alan sniffed more of the white powder from the back of his hand.

"Help us, help us get out of here." Melody stood up and pounded on the door again.

Alan laughed, "Please dear girl, save your breath. You're killing my ears. And believe me, nobody is going to hear you."

The tall blond woman went over to Melody. "The room is completely soundproof. Alan had it built that way. No need for gags in here. It ruins it to put a gag on, then we can't see your face and it ruins part of our enjoyment."

Michael struggled to get free of the chains, but it was useless to even try. With Sybil, it was a game, a sex game, a sort of love ritual, sexually arousing. But here, it was something else. Something weird and sick. With Sybil, Michael was a willing love slave, but here he was their victim. But what sort of victim? This was something else, sordid and horrible and he was starting to get frightened, especially for Melody. If there was only someway to convince them to let her go, but the heroin was starting to make him feel dizzy and lightheaded.

"Now let's see what you're made of," Alan snarled as he took a knife to my pants and cut them off. As he was cutting my shirt off, he stuck me with the knife and I felt the blood trickle down my back.

"Oops, sorry, don't worry, it's not bad, just a nick. I'll be more careful, I promise," he said as he cut off the underwear. Michael was chained there facing the wall, stark naked, just like Eric.

Melody started crying again. "No Melody, that's what they want. Just turn away, don't watch."

But she seemed paralyzed, just standing there against the door, staring at me in disbelief. She wasn't moving at all. She seemed frozen, like a frightened animal caught in the headlights of an oncoming car on a dark road late at night when no one hears your calls for help and, if they do, no one cares.

"Well, Michael, we're going to induct you into our very special society tonight."

"You bastard, what evil are you planning? Why are you doing this. You can stop. You can stop yourselves, right now."

"Ha, ha, ha, that's pretty funny. What fun would that be? Just save your breath. You're going to get what you really came here for." Alan started pressing hard up against Michael.

"No, Alan, I'm warning you to stop."

"Melody finally came back to life screaming, "No Alan, don't do that to Michael!"

"Oh, please, don't give me all that innocent stuff. You knew very well what I was about, didn't you."

"Why don't you tell her what all these marks are all over your back. And Melody, have you seen Michael's engagement ring?" He stepped back so Melody could see Sybil's ring piercing his right nipple, the gold ring with the initial "S" on it.

"I was tied up when they did this to me. It was her," he said pointing to the tall blond woman, "who did that to me. I was tied up and heavily drugged."

"No Melody, don't listen to all his bullshit. He knows my habits. Why don't you ask him why he came here tonight. And why he brought you. He was there in my New York apartment, willingly, with his friend, his patroness, a very wealthy and influential woman. He's here, but really, he belongs to her, like a pet dog."

"I don't belong to anyone," Michael yelled.

"As I was saying, he belongs to her, except when he sneaks off like he did tonight. She doesn't even know he's here. Very, very sneaky, Michael. I don't know how you got away. Clever boy, congratulations. We might as well let all the truth come out tonight. What have we got to hide, anyways."

"Melody, don't believe him. Don't believe one word he says."

"I don't know what to believe anymore."

"It was the drugs, the drugs they were giving me. Don't let them give you any. Never, never take drugs. They do weird things to you. They make everything get all mixed up."

The tall blond woman took Melody by the hand and was leading her over toward us. She helped Melody take off her white tulle dress. She took off Melody's bra and had her step out of her lacy underwear. Melody wasn't even resisting now, she was in some kind of daze, and acted like a mechanical wind-up doll. The tall blond lady was chaining Melody's wrists to the wall, and then her ankles. She was facing out to the room, and Melody just let her. She was totally naked.

"Alan, please don't do this to her. Don't hurt her. She's an innocent. She doesn't deserve this."

"Well, dear boy, it was you who led the lamb here. And there must be something she wanted. I don't think she's all that innocent, do you? Shall we find out?"

"No. Don't you dare touch her."

"Or what? What are you going to do. Come, come now, I don't think you're in any position to help anyone right now, not even yourself."

"Alan, you bastard." Alan was pressing himself against Melody now.

"Come now Melody, what is your fantasy, your deepest darkest secret? What have you imagined during those lonely nights? What have you longed for, for someone to do to you when you knew nobody could read your thoughts, when you weren't afraid to visualize your deepest darkest desires?"

"Alan, do what you want with me, but leave her alone. I'm nothing, do what you want with me, but don't you dare touch her."

"As if you're in any position to dare me to do or not do anything I want!"

Alan ran his hand over her face slowly, feeling every feature of her face. The he stuck his finger in her mouth and ran his other hand down her body. Then he ran both hands down her curves, caressing her all over. She didn't try to resist. She was in a total state of shock. And I couldn't help her. I could only look on helplessly. She was only seventeen, young and fresh and now she was going to be ruined forever.

"Come on, she might even be liking this." Alan moved back over to me after he had his fill of Melody. The blond woman was now starting to run her hands down Melody's body. The older man was watching.

"Alan, you've got to stop this. This isn't a game. You can't do this, hold two people prisoner for your wild sex fantasies. You have to let us go."

"Oh, we'll let you go, all right, when we're good and ready, when we're done with you. You think you can always get what you want. You're the type that never wants to pay your own way. Well, you're going to pay tonight. A few young men tried their little con games on me a long time ago, their cheap little tricks, their lies, but it just doesn't work that way anymore. You have to pay, and pay dearly, pay your dues as you go."

Alan lashed at Michael with a riding crop. Melody shrieked, her poor little body pulsating with fear. Michael thought, if only he could break the chains to his wrists he could stop all this madness.

"If you can guess the real name of our secret society, I'll let your little friend here go."

"I don't believe you. I'm not going to play your stupid games."

Melody screamed, "Guess, Michael, guess!"

"Eric knows, don't you Eric. But, shush, don't tell them. That would really ruin our fun. Eric knows the full impact of those letters, don't you Eric?"

Eric nodded his head up and down, unable to speak.

"Don't tell them Eric, don't let them in on our little secret. We won't, now will we Eric?" Eric nodded again, this time back and forth, no he wouldn't tell them, the dark secret of those initials.

Alan hissed his question over and over again, right in Michael's face, "Secret Society, Secret Society," over and over again. He was so close he was almost touching Michael's lips.

The older man was pressing against Eric now, and the tall blond lady was fondling Melody everywhere, her mouth, her breasts, and her most sensitive places. Then she was kissing Melody on the mouth. Michael couldn't stand to watch anymore, so he turned away. He felt really sick. He had to get her out of there, but how?

"Don't tell them Eric. Don't let them in on our little secret."

The older man suddenly pulled away from Eric, looking startled. Now blood was pouring out of him. Melody was screaming, "Let him down, let him down!"

Both men quickly undid Eric's chains and laid him down on an oriental rug on the floor. Eric was bleeding all over the rug. The rug was turning crimson red.

"Shit, Ernest, I told you to be careful, but you had to go too far, you fucking idiot. This is all I need. There are limits, damn it, limits. And you had to do this here in my house, shit, you fucking lunatic. Why wouldn't listen to me? I warned you before!"

"Alan, what are we going to do now?" The man looked over to Michael and then towards Melody.

Eric wasn't doing too well. He needed help immediately. He was moaning and starting to turn very pale. He was coughing up blood now. He doubled over in pain. He was only in his twenties, and still had so much to live for.

The tall blond woman whacked the man really hard across his face. "You pig, how could you. How could you do this to him!"

"Can't someone get a doctor, get a doctor here quick. Call 911, get an ambulance here!" Michael yelled. "Can't you see he's going down fast."

"Come on, there's no time for this. We've got to think what to do."

"What do you mean, he's probably dying. You got to get him help fast." Michael couldn't believe they weren't calling for help.

Eric was coughing softer now and then the coughing stopped. He turned blue, shuddered and then stopped moving altogether.

"Shit, you've really done it, you've gone and really done it this time. What are we going to do now?" Alan was beside himself.

"Oh shit, Alan, the police. We've got to get him out of here." The man was really sweating now. "And what about those two?"

The tall blond woman shouted, "No, let them go. Isn't this enough for one night to deal with?"

"But," Alan protested, "We can't just let them go. They saw, they saw what happened!"

"It was an accident, wasn't it, Ernest? Nobody intended for this to happen, a freak accident," the tall blond woman wanted Ernest to answer.

"Yes, it was an accident, he said softly now like he really meant it. But what about them?" he pointed to Melody and Michael.

"Just let them go, why complicate things. Let them go. They won't say anything, will you," the tall blond woman wanted them to answer.

"Sure, it's easy for you to say, you're not the one who did it. It's not your neck on the line," Ernest was getting worked up again.

The tall blond woman started to unchain Melody and then handed her the white tulle dress and her other clothes. "Here you better put these on. You won't say anything, will you?"

"NO. Never!" Melody screamed. "Just let me out of here."

"Sure, sure, she's going to say whatever we want, so we'll let her go. We can't believe them. We don't know what they're going to do the minute they get out of here." Ernest said angrily.

While all this arguing was going on, Eric was just lying on the rug motionless. Finally Alan walked over to him, took a long mournful look, and then threw half the rug over the lifeless body.

Alan came over to Michael, "What about you, Michael. Are going to say anything about our problem here tonight, the accident? We can't let any of this out, can we? It would ruin all of us, the publicity. We'd be ruined. It would be all over. Even you, just the fact that you were here."

"But it's all over for Eric, isn't it, with your stupid hideous games." Michael shouted.

"No Michael, say you won't say anything," Melody begged.

"If we do let you go, and if you talk to anyone, anyone at all, all three of us will say it was you who did it. Michael, do you understand?"

"They won't believe you. There's the evidence."

"Listen to me. Who are they going to believe three well established, respected pillars of the community, or a worthless drifter, a gigolo like you."

"I'm not a gigolo."

"Remember Michael, in this country money is power, and money can buy just about anything, even the justice system."

"Especially out here. We practically own some of the judges." Ernest added.

"Shut up, Ernest, you're always putting your foot in it." Alan shouted.

"If we let you go, Michael, you won't say anything, will you?" Alan carefully freed one of Michael's wrists from the handcuff. Then he leant down and released both ankles.

"Say No, Michael," Melody screamed hysterically. "Say you won't talk to anybody about this."

"I have an idea," Alan grabbed a bottle of Johnny Walker Red. He took a handkerchief and carefully wiped the entire bottle with it. Alan handed the bottle to Michael who took it. Then Alan wrapped the bottle in a towel, careful not to touch it. He picked up Eric's belt off the floor. It had a metal buckle on it with a big turquoise stone. Alan wiped Eric's belt and the buckle down with a towel. Then Alan handed Eric's belt to Michael. "Here, hold this by the buckle."

Michael figured if he humored him, just maybe he would let them get out of there alive.

"Sure Alan, whatever you say.

Alan wrapped the belt, careful not to touch it.

"Here, Michael, why don't you try on these nice Ray Ban sunglasses."

Michael put them on.

"No, they're not a gift. I need those back too."

Michael handed them back to Alan who wrapped the Ray Bans in tissue paper without touching them.

"Eric's. We'll keep all these here for safekeeping." Alan opened a floor board and there was a safe just below. Alan put all three objects in the safe, the whiskey bottle, the belt with its buckle and the Ray Ban sunglasses. Then he turned the dial and closed the floor board. "Just in case you get any ideas to destroy the evidence, the evidence of what you did to Eric.

"What? What are you talking about?"

"Yes, our little insurance policy, in case you change your mind about talking. And what about Sybil? She won't be happy, no, not at all, about your cute little friend you obviously care so much about. No, Michael, she won't like that at all. I wouldn't want to be in your shoes if she finds out, especially after all she's done for you."

"No, you're right, she can't find out, about any of this."

"I don't think she'll take it too well. I don't think you'll ever work in film or stage, ever, east or west coast. She's got quite a bit of influence, you know,"

"What about the girl. We can't trust her, we can't count on her silence," Ernest sounded concerned.

"No, I suppose you're right." Alan eyed her carefully.

"The little rat would squeal the minute she got home, or maybe the minute she got out of here," Ernest continued.

"I won't, I promise," Melody pleaded.

"Ernest is right. We better think about her." Alan looked worried.

"No, I won't leave without her."

"Michael, you have to leave. Sybil will be looking for you by morning. And if you call anyone, it's you who will be endangering her life. We have a lot at stake here, all of us."

Alan undid the last handcuff and then threw Michael a pile of clothes from the floor. "Here put these on. Yours are in shreds."

Michael rubbed his wrists and put on the clothes. He thought, if he got out of there, he could get help for Melody. They're obviously not going to release her, at least not for now. But he tried one more time, "Just let her go with me. I'll get her out of here and back to New York. You'll never see or hear of her again."

"Nice try Michael. We'll decide what's going on here, all right?"

"Michael, go ahead, you have to leave right now. I'll be alright."

Michael finished dressing and slipped on his shoes, the Armani loafers.

"We're going to let her go. We just don't want you two leaving together. In case you get any brains storms about this and not think of your future, your future in anything." Ernest threatened.

"O.K. Ernest is right. We're going to let her go. We just have to think this out a little more carefully, that's all. We'll figure something out," Alan said, not all that reassuringly.

"Michael, go, get out of here while you can."

"Melody, I can't leave you here."

"Yes, you have to go. It's no good us both being here."

Alan opened a door, not the one that led to the screening room, but one that opened onto a stairway.

Michael took one last look at Melody, "I'm sorry, I didn't mean to get you mixed up in all this."

"Michael it's time to go. Go up the stairway. It will lead you to the back garden. Just follow the path to the rear gate. I'll buzz you through. Don't try anything. We have security cameras everywhere. Then keep going straight, turn left, second right, and soon you'll be on Sybil's road."

"Sybil's? You're going back to Sybil?"

Michael couldn't answer.

"And don't forget Michael, not a word to anyone, not even Sybil. It's your word against ours and I've got your fingerprints all over everything."

Michael took a long last look at Melody and left. He quickly climbed the stairs and found himself outside in the garden.

"What else could I do, what choices did I have?" he thought. He would stay close by and see if they released her. He'd hide just beyond the rear gate. If they didn't let her go after a short while, he'd go and get help. That was a comforting thought, but as he was nearing the gate, he heard them coming, dogs, two huge vicious snarling dogs. They looked like wolves, baring their white gleaming fangs. They were snarling ferocious monsters and were running right towards him. They were coming straight at him. He jumped up onto the gate, but now they were snapping at his feet. They were just about to tear one foot off, but they got one of his shoes instead. They were mangling his Armani loafer, and then
they started fighting over it. Michael wondered if they were let loose on purpose to finish him off, or did they just forget about the dogs in all the excitement? Michel managed to climb over the top of the gate and jump down to the other side. He left the dogs snarling at him through the gate. Then they lifted their heads up

and started howling, making a horrible racket. No one was getting near Alan's place tonight.

Michael thought he could watch the house from just beyond the gate, if only the damn dogs would quiet down. He tried to stand motionless next to some trees, but no such luck. The dogs wouldn't shut up. Then a light went on in the neighbor's house just several yards away across a dirt road. He hoped there wouldn't be another set of dogs. That's all he needed now. No, it was just the man of the house coming out onto his porch. He was holding something in his hands. It was a big hunting rifle. He looked around and then the man started yelling, "If there's a son of a bitch on my property, I'm going to blow his fucking head right off."

Michael crept away as quietly as he could. No dogs this time, just one mad dog. Now he wouldn't be able to watch Alan's house after all. Michael started to shake and he felt feverish. He was sweating even though the night air was cold. He couldn't even think anymore. He just found himself heading back to Sybil's house, not really knowing what he was doing.

He found his way back to her place and snuck quietly up the driveway, staying close to the hedges to stay well out of sight. He got back in the way he came out. He climbed the tree and swung over the gutter and into the window that he had left ajar.

He was relieved to see no one had touched anything in the room. It was just exactly the way he had left it, the bed with the towels under the cover, the new clothes spread everywhere. And the door was still locked from the inside. He removed the towels, unlocked the door and crept out onto the landing. He walked towards Sybil's room. He just had to see someone. The door to her room was unlocked. Then he saw there was someone asleep in Sybil's bed, right next to her. It was Cecil. He got out of there as fast as he could and hightailed it back to his room. He locked the door and climbed into bed. He was too tired to move and he passed out dressed in the clothes Alan had given him.

He dreamed a heavy dream and had visions of hell. He was burning. Then he woke up with a start. But this was hell, he was already there. Hell was what went on in Alan's house. Hell was not knowing what was happening to Melody. And he thought, "Hell was being me."

CHAPTER 13 - Tuesday, August 5

Riverhead Correctional Facility

When I finished telling the lawyer the story, he looked at me with a very strange look. I don't think he believed one word I told him about that night.

"Are you sure that's exactly how it happened, the murder of Eric Brennan?"

"I'm telling you the truth, in exact detail, just like you asked me. You've got to help me get out of this."

"Well, it's not going to be easy, but I'll do the best I can for you."

"Funny, you don't sound very convincing."

"As soon as I review your file, I'll let you know what kind of defenses we have. I've ordered a psychiatric evaluation. It could help your case."

"I'm not nuts."

"No, but with that confession, I need to look at this as a possibility. You'll need to cooperate if you want me to help you."

He picked up his briefcase and banged on the door. The guard came and let him out. The door shut with the ring of hopeless finality.

Then the guard came back and led me to my cell. Herman asked how it went.

"I don't know. He's a damn public defender. I heard about those guys."

"Yeah, I got one myself. He hasn't done much for me yet, as far as I can see. Why don't you tell me about the night you were arrested and how they got that confession out of you."

"I told you I didn't confess. I really don't remember too much after the arrest. All I know is they grilled me for hours, right through the night. I'll start with the morning after I got back from Alan's, that horrible night and maybe it will come back to me."

"It was Sunday, August 3, the morning after I got back from Alan's. I woke with a start. I was in my room at Sybil's beach house in East Hampton. I was in a heavy sweat. I was burning up. I walked over and opened the window all the way and stuck my head out to take in a deep breath of fresh air. It was the fresh air of early morning blowing in off the ocean. It's amazing, everything looked the same outside. The trees had green leaves, the sky was blue and the birds were singing. Nothing in the universe seemed to care about the tragedy of last night. It was if nothing had even happened.

I walked over to the mirror in the bathroom and splashed cold water on my face. Shit, I was still wearing Eric's clothes! Melody must have made it home by now, I thought to reassure myself. The last I saw her, she was still in that room at Alan's house, pleading with me to leave, to leave her there. She was right, there was no sense in us both being there after they agreed to let me go. I don't know, it seemed logical at the time, but now everything seems messed up. I was supposed to get help, but somehow it didn't work out like that and here I am back at Sybil's. I must have passed out and now it's morning. I wonder what time it is. Shit. Eight A.M. It must be the drugs Alan gave me. I've got to get to a phone and call her apartment. I have to know if she made it home. She must be there by now, but she can't call me here. She doesn't even know the number. How could she. And of course there's no phone in my room. Only in Sybil's room and the kitchen where Maria always seems to be.

I took off Eric's clothes, his blue shirt and khaki trousers and balled them up. I hid them in the back pouch of my suitcase and put it back on the top shelf in the closet. I wasn't feeling too good. I was a little unsteady on my feet. I still felt dizzy. I quickly showered and put on the red terry cloth robe and got back into bed. I never wanted to try drugs again, never, especially not with strangers. It all seemed like a bad dream, maybe even a drug induced hallucination. Maybe Eric wasn't really dead. Maybe I just imagined they killed Eric.

Just as I was settling back into bed under the warm down comforter and about to fall back asleep, the door opened. It was Sybil. She crawled into bed with me, gave me an affectionate kiss and just held me. It felt good.

"Sleep well last night? I hope so 'cause we have quite a morning ahead of us. Remember we're off to Montauk for an early morning ride."

"Sybil, I don't know if I can. I don't feel too well. I think I have a fever or something."

"Here, let me feel your forehead. You might be right. It feels like you're burning up. I better send for Maria and have her take your temperature."

Sybil got out of bed and went to get Maria.

Several minutes later Maria came into the room carrying a silver tray with a large glass of orange juice and a bottle of aspirins. Under her arm was a newspaper, the thick Sunday edition.

"I hear not feeling too well this morning, Seignor. Here, let me take your temperature."

"No, don't bother, Maria, I'll be all right. No need to fuss over me."

"No fuss, besides it's Madame's orders."

"I opened my mouth and let Maria play nurse. She also took my pulse. Then after a few minutes she looked at the mercury and pointed a finger at me. Seignor better stay in bed today. Small temperature. Here, drink this."

She handed me the fresh orange juice and then took two aspirins out of the bottle. "Seignor, take these, to bring the temperature down. I weel come back with your breakfast."

She handed me the newspaper, picked up the tray and left the room. That was nice, being taken care of like that. I opened the newspaper. Then I saw it, big as day and right on Page One, a photograph of a burned out car. The headline in big black bold letters across the top of the page read, "TERRIBLE CAR ACCIDENT IN EAST HAMPTON LAST NIGHT. Two bodies found in wreckage."

When I read on, I felt sick to my stomach.

"No positive ID's have been made yet of the two bodies found inside. The bodies were burned beyond recognition, but one is believed to be a male and the other a female."

Then it went on to say how long it took to put out the fire and extricate the bodies.

"Police are checking the registration of the car, a blue 1989 Buick, and are looking for any evidence they can find at the scene. No other vehicles seem to have been involved that we know of at this time. The bodies are being sent to forensics and identification will be attempted from dental records. At this time police believe it might be a simple story of two people out on a Saturday night with the driver being drunk and losing control of the vehicle. The Buick crashed into a large tree and exploded with the passengers trapped inside. An empty bottle of Johnny Walker Red was found on the side of the road near the crash site. The time of the accident is estimated at approximately four A.M. It appears that the car may have exploded on impact. Anyone having any information about the accident or possible identification of the victims is asked to call the East Hampton police at the toll free number 1-800-329-7209."

I couldn't read anymore. No! It couldn't be Melody. She had to be home by now. I'll call her apartment when we go out. I'll insist I'm better and make Sybil take us to lunch at the Yacht Club. I've got to find out for sure. Melody is probably sound asleep in her nice little bed back in Queens. No everything's fine. Nothing happened to her last night.

Then I looked at the photos on the front page again. It was hard to make out with the grainy newsprint. A police officer was holding something in his hand and looking at it. It looked like a scarf. No, it was impossible. He was holding Melody white scarf in his hand. But it couldn't be. Those bastards, they killed her. And then they got rid of Eric's body at the same time.

Bastards! They made it look like a couple out for a Saturday night with a drunk driver. An accident to cover up an accident. But it could be anything. Maybe it wasn't Melody. Maybe the scarf flew out the window as they were having her driven home. But I knew. I was just fooling myself. Was she trying leave a sign? Did she throw the scarf out of the window before the car exploded? Did she know she was going to her death? The article said a white scarf was found several yards from the wreckage. It was all too horrible to think about. Was she alive and conscious when it happened? I had to know. I had to know everything. The pain of thinking about that night was too much and I let out an agonizing cry.

Sybil came rushing into my room. "Michael, are you all right? Shall I call a doctor?"

"No, a doctor can't help me."

"I'll cancel the horseback riding. We'll do it another time. I can use the time to stay here and catch up on my work."

"Really Sybil, I'm feeling much better now. I need to get out of here and get some fresh air. Let's go to the Yacht Club for lunch. Come on, what do you say. I hate to ruin all your plans for today."

"Well, if you're well enough to go to the Yacht Club, we should go horseback riding on the beach at Montauk. The Yacht Club doesn't open for another four hours anyways. So we might as well take off before there's people on the beach at Montauk."

"O.K. Sybil, if that's the plan."

"Great, I hate to cancel the horses. And it's my last chance before we start filming to get out for a nice early morning ride."

I dressed quickly. Shit. When I went to put my shoes on, I knew I was in deep trouble. I had to keep Sybil from noticing one of my Armani loafers was missing. Then I remembered the dogs. I hoped the dogs had totally eaten it and didn't leave any scraps. I couldn't wear my old Dingos or the dress shoes I wore to the costume ball. Then I remembered the boating shoes Sybil bought me and took them out of box.

We rode to Montauk in Sybil's red Jeep. The roads were much

quieter today. The view of the ocean was so beautiful but all I wanted to do was cry. The seagulls were screaming and making a horrible racket swooping over the sand. How could it look so beautiful and everything be so wrong. I tried to control it. I couldn't let Sybil see me so upset.

"Michael, what's the matter. What's wrong with you? Are you O.K? You've been so quiet this morning."

"No, it's nothing. It'll pass."

"Michael, tell me, what is this all about."

"I don't know. I don't know what it's about," I lied as I tried to get myself under control. I pictured how beautiful she looked as she stepped off the train in that white tulle dress. It kept flashing with the image of her chained and naked in that room, being molested first by Alan and then the tall blond woman. I was torturing myself with those images that kept flashing back and forth in my mind.

Sybil drove us out to a far point in Montauk. There were two horses waiting for us. Sybil stripped down to a tiny bikini and told me to just wear my briefs. We mounted the two roan horses and rode along the wide sandy beach. It was so beautiful but I still felt sick to my stomach. Sybil got off her horse in a deserted cove on the beach. She did look so incredible as she lay on her back and shielded her eyes from the sun. I crept up on her and had to have her right then. I pulled her bikini down and we had mad passionate sex right there on the beach. I don't know how long it went on, but finally we both came together in a wild orgasm, throbbing together. Then we sat there for a few minutes as we looked out at the surf rolling in. We both dressed and got back on the horses and returned to Sybil's red jeep. A groom was waiting to take the horses back to the stable.

"I'm famished. How about you?" Sybil looked at her diamond Rolex watch.

"Yes, let's go straight to the Yacht Club. O.K.?"

"Well, by the time we get there, it will be open."

Soon we were pulling up to the restaurant. The next edition of the paper was out. It had a different headline. I read it through the vending machine window, "BODIES AT CRASH SCENE IDENTIFIED."

While Sybil headed inside to get us a table, I got a paper and read the headlines outside before going in. "A young man and woman tragically ended their lives last night when their vehicle crashed into a tree in East Hampton."

I joined Sybil at a table overlooking the pier lined with small yachts bobbing about on the grey choppy waters. A waiter came over and handed us two oversized menus. I started reading the article, "It appears the young man, the driver, was heavily intoxicated and lost control of the vehicle. The woman has been identified as seventeen year old Melody Anderson of Queens. She leaves behind her parents, Margaret and Dean Anderson, also of Queens, and an older sister from Washington, D.C. The man's next of kin have not been notified so his name is being withheld at this time."

"Michael, I've been asking you three times what do you want to order?"

I had no desire to eat, but I ordered eggs benedict and two mimosas because Sybil insisted. Sybil began chatting with a couple she knew at the next table. Melody Anderson, I didn't even know her last name. Fuck, if I didn't say anything, it looked like Alan and his friends were going to get away with murder, double murder. I couldn't let that happen. I had to think fast. And as long as they were free, I was in danger, danger from their blackmail threats to frame me for what they did. What if they thought I wasn't safe anymore, that my conscience was getting to me, that I was going to talk.

The waiter brought over our brunch and the drinks, but I couldn't eat one bite of it. Poor Sybil, she didn't know any of this. Why had I strayed from her, why had I cheated on her. She's been so good to me. Why did I sneak out on her last night and betray her? Why couldn't I just be content with all the great things she was doing for me? Why do I always have to fuck everything up?

"Michael, come on, you'd better snap out of it. Your food is getting cold."

"Excuse me, Sybil, I have to rush down to the men's room. I don't feel well."

I went downstairs and saw the phone. I had to dial Melody's number, hoping maybe her parents were there. I would tell them, without giving my name, and they could tell the police what really happened. I dialed her number.

A man answered, "Hello, who is this?" I heard automated clicks in the background, like the call was being recorded.

"Who is this? Is this Melody's father?"

"What's your name? Do you know anything about last night?"

It sounded like the police. They were at her apartment.

"No, I don't know what you're talking about."

"We need information..."

I hung up the phone before they could trace the call. I ran up the stairs and hurried back to Sybil's table. She was already signing the receipt.

"We have to get back. Annize is coming over."

When we got back, I went straight to my room. It would only be a matter of time, I thought, before they linked Eric to Alan. Everyone at the party saw them together around the pool at the party. But people saw me with Melody! I still had to get rid of Eric's clothes that were in the suitcase in the closet. I was in a very dangerous position and I didn't know what to do. I couldn't bear the pain any more, the loss of Melody, the flashing images of that night came back, the horrible images of her throwing the scarf out of the car window and her burning up in the fire. She's gone and I'm the one responsible for it. She was only seventeen and I was her first lover.

I can't possibly tell Sybil. I felt truly alone. I knelt down next to the bed, like my aunt made me do when I was a child. I hated her for it. You can't force someone to pray. But for the first time in my life, I prayed. I needed to find the answer to all this evil out of control, but I knew we had to suffer for our own sins. We had to suffer before we could find any meaning, any way out of this horrible confusion of evil and self and flesh. I had come fact-to-face with evil, real evil, of man descended to his most animal-like self. That was the devil, the animal in us out of control. That we could allow ourselves to descend to such depths. We had to rise, to stand upright and act upright, look to a higher plane, through the spirit, and fight the flesh and the animal in us, our demons. I wanted to fight it, to resist, but look where all this led, to this damnation, to this hell!

I knew I led her to her torture and to her death. I couldn't bear to think about it. We take the innocent with us when to go down the wrong path. I took her down with me, but it was she who perished. There must be a purpose, a reason to this existence.

I got up from the floor and crawled into bed. I still had all the answers to find and none of the questions I needed to find them. As I lay back in bed, I thought I now knew what that scene meant, the one from Hamlet that we had to memorize for class at the Institute. I knew exactly what Hamlet meant when he said, "To be or not to be, that is the question, whether 'tis nobler in the mind to suffer the slings and arrows of outrageous fortune" (to do nothing against Alan and his sicko friends) "or to take arms against a sea of troubles and by opposing end them" (go to the police and take the fucking consequences). "To die to sleep no more and by sleep to say we end the heartache and a thousand natural shocks that flesh is heir to" (no, I will never try to kill myself.) "Tis a consummation devoutly to be wished, to die to sleep, to sleep, perchance to dream." I wish I could just sleep and dream and not have any more of those hellish nightmares. Tomorrow I will decide what to do. Tomorrow I will take action. Tomorrow.

CHAPTER 14 - Monday, August 4, East Hampton

Sybil and I had coffee the next morning, just like nothing had ever happened.

"Cecil won't be here today to drive me to the first location. She had to leave very early this morning. Her mother died Saturday. Poor thing. She was so distraught after that phone call last night, she didn't want to be alone, so she asked if she could sleep in my bed, just like a little kid. I didn't have the heart to refuse her. She's been with me for five years. She took a plane out early this morning to go home to Minneapolis for her mother's funeral. She'll be back in a few days."

I could hardly contain my enthusiasm for hearing about Cecil's mother's funeral. Of course that explained them sleeping together in Sybil's bed. I hadn't seen them do anything. They were both sound asleep, but I just assumed. I was so happy I just got up and wrapped my arms around Sybil, almost spilling her coffee. Suddenly I got my appetite back and started to eat the huevos rancheros Maria left out for us on the table.

"Michael, you're so unpredictable. Are you feeling better today? You didn't eat a thing yesterday. Are you well enough to go on location with me? It's totally different than shooting on a sound stage. There we can control the elements, but on location, we have to deal with the unpredictable. That's what makes shooting on a sound stage so great. But shooting on location makes the movie seem more real, dogs barking, ambient noise of crickets and birds, real locations. Of course we can add that to the sound track, but it's not the same. But when localities change their rules on us when we're trying pull permits, it's a real headache. Are you ready to go, and then we're going to have lunch with Alan. I have to talk to him about getting financing for my next project."

"I can't go, Sybil."

"But I want you there,"

"No, Sybil, I still don't feel up to it. I just can't go. I need to go back to bed."

"You don't know what you're missing. Shooting on location is great and there's so much you can learn from watching today."

"I'm really not up to it, believe me."

"But you can be a big help to me. There's always something going wrong and there's never enough people to fix it. You really don't look that sick to me."

Maria came into the breakfast room, "Madame there's a call for you. It's Alan." She handed the phone to Sybil.

"Alan, how are you. Not too good? That's too bad. What? You can't make lunch today. You're not trying to get out of our deal, are you, for the next picture? What! Something terrible happened. An accident. A car accident with Eric? Eric's dead! You just found out it was him in the car. The car they found early Sunday morning? Oh, how terrible for you. I know you were very fond of him, and were grooming him to be your next assistant. How did it happen? He left your party Saturday night late with another guest? A girl from New York. I'm terribly sorry, Alan. O.K. I understand. We'll make it another time.

I better let you go or you're going to miss that flight. I'll see you when you get back from LA. Take care, Alan."

"Michael, that was Alan. He won't be making it for lunch after all. Eric's dead. He's the boy in that horrible car crash. Alan is sick about it. He must be devastated. He's flying out on business to L.A. right now."

"Alan is sick all right. He's an evil, sick man, Sybil. He needs help. He needs to be behind bars."

"What the hell are you talking about?"

"He's all twisted inside and now he's walking out of here, just like that. Well, he said he was rich and powerful and could control all this, and I guess he was right."

"What?"

"I was there, Sybil, I was there at Alan's house Saturday night."

"That's impossible."

"Yes, I couldn't stay in my room, so I snuck out and went to

Alan's party. It was innocent enough, sort of, except I knew the girl, Melody. And Eric didn't die in that crash. He died in Alan's house."

"Michael, you're crazy. I don't want to hear any more of this."

"It's true, Sybil. You just don't want to hear the truth. Alan is involved. I can't go into it all right now. I have to figure out what to say to the police, and I don't want you to be involved in any of this."

"The police? What are you talking about?"

"Yes, I made up my mind last night. I can't hide it anymore."

"But Michael, you were here at the time of the accident."

"Yes, that's right."

"Maria saw you creeping down the hallway at about 3:00 A.M. She told me. Alan said the car crash was about 4:00 in the morning. You couldn't have been there. You were here."

"Bless Maria and her snoopy ways."

"She thought you were a burglar and almost shot you. She

said she recognized you just in time, just before pulling the trigger. It was aimed right at your head. She thought you were a burglar about to go into my room and hurt me, but good thing you turned around just in time. Then she saw it was you."

"Bless Maria."

"What, you lunatic. She almost killed you and you're saying that? I didn't want to tell you. I thought it would upset you."

"Upset? That's the best thing I've heard all day. That's my alibi. Maria saw me here at 3:00 A.M and almost shot me. I had just gotten back from Alan's."

"You should never have gone there. I never go to his parties out here. They get too wild, too out of hand."

"That wasn't out of hand in New York?"

"No, he's much worse out here."

"Sybil, he killed someone Saturday night."

"What are you talking about?"

"He killed the girl after his friend killed Eric."

"Michael, you're mad! They died in a car accident."

"No, they didn't."

"I don't know what you're talking about. Alan is a very good friend and he's helped me so much. I think the fever is affecting your brain. You need medical attention and I'm going to make sure you get it. I have to go now. I'm due on location in thirty minutes. I've hired a driver for the week while Cecil is away. You stay here and rest. I'll see you when I get back. And believe me, you need plenty of rest."

"But Sybil . . . "

She hurried out of the dining room, but took one look back at me in disbelief.

I had to get over to Alan's house. He should have left for L.A. by now. I had to have a look around, try to see if I could find my other loafer, or what was left of it, and the belt and Ray Bans with my prints all over them. I had to find them before the police did, or worse, before Alan got nervous and turned them over to the police. I had to find something, I didn't know what. I was hoping the police hadn't run the fingerprints on the bottle they found on the side of the road.

I waited 'til I saw Sybil's limo pull out of the driveway. Then I hurried downstairs and retraced my steps back to Alan's house, just exactly as I went there last Saturday night.

Once I got there, I climbed over the rear gate very carefully. That neighbor didn't seem to be there and luckily Alan's dogs were nowhere in sight. He must have locked them up or put them in a kennel before he left for L.A. Nobody seemed to be around. I entered through a window at the rear of the house and slipped as silently as I could down the stairway, along the gallery of black paintings, past the screening room and into the room where they murdered poor Eric. Now there was furniture everywhere covered with white linen throws, sofas, a dozen dining room chairs, a large old crystal chandelier on the floor, and all kinds of junk. I had to find something that I could bring to the police so they would believe me. It was my word against theirs, all three of them, plus Alan's butler. He'd no doubt back up whatever Alan told him to say. Now that makes four against one.

I pushed the sofa aside to find the trap door that hid the safe. It opened easily enough, but it was empty. Of course, Alan had already removed everything from the safe. I looked around. No, nobody would ever guess what the real purpose of this room had been just two nights ago. Now it was just a storage room. The chains had no doubt been removed from the wall. An ornate gilded mirror and two large old landscape paintings hung over the places where they had been secured.

I walked into the screening room and looked around. Just as I was about to leave, I noticed a light coming from the projection booth. Very slowly I approached and carefully opened the door.

It was Alan. He looked up from the film he had been studying with a magnifying glass. Our eyes locked in disbelief.

"Hey, you're not supposed to be here."

"Neither are you."

He started moving towards me. I punched him as hard as

I could. He fought back. Alan was in good shape and he got me in a corner until I landed one good punch square to his jaw that sent him sprawling to the floor. "That's for Melody and here's one for me." I hit him again as he tried to get up. I kicked him. "And that one's for Eric."

"Stop it, stop it. What the hell are you doing here?"

"I thought you were on your way to L.A."

"No, that's just what the police were told. They wanted to question me."

Alan lifted himself up and sat down on the chair. "But I'm not quite ready for them, yet. And Ernest is just about to lift off for L.A. right now, with an airline ticket in my name. We thought it best if he left town for awhile. Have you told anyone yet?"

"Only Sybil and she won't believe me."

"No, Michael," he laughed, "No one's going to believe you. And if you're a smart boy, you'll quit while you're ahead. Don't talk to anybody. Believe me it's in your best interest."

"Alan, where's all that stuff with my fingerprints on it."

"Wouldn't you like to know. Come on now, that's our insurance policy. Against you."

"Why did you kill poor innocent Melody?"

"That was an accident."

"Sure, with Eric's body in it."

"No, you don't understand. She stole the butler's car, trying to get away."

"Sure, she drove off with Eric's body."

"We had Eric's body in it, to dispose of, so to speak. Then we went back in the house to take a good last look around, to make sure all that dreadful mess was cleaned up. In the confusion, we left Melody alone in the backseat of the car. The keys were already in the ignition and Melody seized the opportunity to try to get away. Well, naturally we had to follow her, to get her, the car and Eric's body back before she could get to the police with it. So there was a high speed chase. We were all going too fast and well, she must have lost control and crashed into the tree. I'm sure you know the rest from the papers."

"Alan, somehow I don't believe a word you just said."

"Who cares." He poured himself a vodka on the rocks, clinking the ice cubes into a glass with a pair of silver tongs.

"I think you and your friends put Eric's poor dead body in the car, doused him with whiskey, forced Melody into the passenger seat, and made it look like Eric drove into the tree. You made the car explode and knew the fire would get rid of all the evidence."

Alan was silent.

"Of course, I know that's exactly what happened. You would never let Melody out of your sight, not with the three of you. Plus the butler. And she would never have the nerve to take the car."

"Whatever. And anyways, what you think doesn't matter." Alan gulped down more of the vodka.

"How can you be so cold about all this, and you don't even care about the police."

"We planned ahead. I think we have the situation well in hand. That is if you don't spoil it. We all have to repeat the same story, if questioned. That's all. That they just left together, the two of them and borrowed the butler's car. And Eric was drunk. That's the way we'll tell it to the police." Alan took another sip, this time directly from bottle, Grey Goose Vodka. Only the best for him, just like he said the other night.

"Actually, I'm glad you came over. Now we can all have the same story. Unless you'd like a different version, the one that implicates you in everything."

"Alan, you're an evil wicked man."

"So I'm told." He took another slug from the bottle.

"I'm not helping you in your cover up."

"Suit yourself."

"Why do you sound so calm, like you could care less."

"What we're involved with here, Michael, is called damage control."

"It's a little too late for that, isn't it?"

"Now Michael, you're not going to do anything foolish, are you? Remember, you're involved in this as much as we are, only more so."

"I know Alan, you're planning to frame me for Eric's murder."

"Accident, dear boy."

"And somehow, I suspect you're going to frame me for Melody, too."

"Well, let's just put it this way, you're not so innocent as to Melody."

"What do you mean by that?"

"You're not too clever, or at least you're not as clever as you think you are. It's your shoe, your Armani loafer or rather what's left of it by the time the dogs got finished nibbling on that fine Italian leather, the one we retrieved from Mac and Moe."

"Mac and Moe. The two wolf dogs?"

"Malamutes to you."

"Go on."

"Well, we put what was left of your shoe in the trunk of the car."

"But . . . "

"We had to take precautions. We figured if anything survived the blaze, there'd better be something belonging to you in that car."

"So now, you're trying to pin that one on me too. And I thought you said Melody stole the car."

"Oh, she did."

"Alan, you're totally contradicting yourself. Everything you say is a lie. I'm getting out of here right now."

"Oh no you're not. I've been ringing for Sydney."

"Who's that?"

"The butler, and a very good black belt too. He kind of doubles as my bodyguard around here."

Just then, the doorbell rang. Alan pressed the intercom to listen. It was the police. Sydney the butler was upstairs. We both listened in as Sydney opened the front door.

"Good day gentlemen. What can I do for you?"

"Is Mr. Prescott in?"

"No, I'm afraid not. He left about two hours ago for Los Angeles. Urgent business on the West Coast."

"That's too bad. We have some questions we want to ask him. About his party here last Saturday night."

"Well I'll be sure to inform him of that. He'll be back in a few days. I'm not sure where he's staying."

"Be sure he calls the number on this card as soon as he gets back. Do you mind if we have a look around? It'll only take a few minutes."

"I'm afraid I can't let you in without Mr. Prescott's permission. I'm not allowed to let anyone in while he's away. Unless of course you have a search warrant."

"No, we don't have a warrant. Is anyone else here?"

"No, just myself."

"Be sure to tell him to call me as soon as he gets back."

"Yes, I will do that. Have a nice day." Sidney looked down at the card.

Alan turned off the intercom. "See Michael, damage control. I'll have my own people over here within the hour to go over this place with a fine tooth comb. And when those two do come back, with their little detective bag of tricks, we'll have gotten rid of any little specks of suspicious evidence. They'll just find what we want them to find. Nothing. Peace, order, harmony. It really is a very tranquil place here, don't you think?"

"Alan, it looks like you've taken care of just about everything."

"Everything except you, of course. You're the one loose cannon still walking around. If Sybil wasn't so damn fond of you... She'd be sure to miss you, especially at night. Only joking. Now be a good lad and everything will go exactly as planned and nobody gets involved."

"Alan, you're disgusting. You're not going to get away with this. They'll find out what really happened eventually."

"Always the optimist."

"I'll see you in hell Alan."

I slammed the door to the projection room and ran upstairs. I stepped back out through the window just as Sydney entered the room. I ran across the grounds, but Sydney didn't seem to be following me. I guess Alan thought he had everything very neatly under control. And that bothered me.

The fever was coming back, and so was the nausea. As soon as I got back to Sybil's house, I undressed and got back into bed. I had to think. There was nothing I could do but wait until Sybil returned home, and then try to get her help telling the police. I was going to need all the help I could get, against Alan and his army of liars, his money, and all his connections.

As soon as I was peacefully settled into bed, Maria came padding down the hallway and came into my room. "I'm sorry to bother you, Seignor, but there are two policemen downstairs. They are insisting you come down. They said they want to ask you some questions."

"Maria, try to reach Sybil, right now!"

"Oh, I can't, Seignor. She's filming on location today, and she said they're on a very tight schedule."

"Well try."

"O.K. but all I can do is leave a message for her to call back."

"Tell her it's urgent," I told her as I put on my jeans and shirt.

"Very well, Seignor. You'd better hurry. They said if you didn't come down right away, they would come up and get you."

I finished putting on my old dingo boots as quickly as I could and hurried downstairs. They were waiting in the entry.

"Michael Connell?"

"Yes?"

"We're placing you under arrest."

"What!"

"For the murder of Eric Brennan. You have the right to remain silent. Anything you say can and will be used against you. You have a right to an attorney and if you can't hire one, an attorney will be appointed for you."

"I need to call Sybil."

"Call them from the stationhouse. I have to take you in and book you. Turn around, put your hands behind your back." The officer put handcuffs on.

"They're too tight."

"Tell it to the judge," he laughed.

"Hey Jack, go search the place. Which one is your room?"

"Don't you need a search warrant?"

"Wise guy, huh. How'd you like to arrive with your face still in one piece."

"Hey Jack, go to his room. Start there. The maid will take you. Then just tear it apart."

He led me outside to the police car and patted me down.

"Hey you, get in, and watch your head. I wish they'd let us at scumbags like you."

"Aren't I innocent till proven guilty. I didn't do anything."

"Tell it to the judge, you little fuck. And you'd better have a damn good lawyer."

They took me down to the local precinct and booked me in, fingerprinted me, took pictures, front and side, and asked if I had a record anywhere.

"Any prior offenses?"

"No."

"Date of birth, social security number."

Then they took me to a little room, and sat me down in a chair. They started asking questions. They asked where I was from, where I'd been the last five years, the last week, Saturday night, today. And if I had a statement to make.

"A statement about what?"

"About the two people you were seen leaving the party with. The party last Saturday night. Remember, at Alan Prescott's house."

"I didn't leave the party with anyone, not with those two people."

"So you admit you were there, with the victims, and you knew them."

"I knew them, but I'm telling you, I left by myself."

"Oh really, would you like to elaborate."

"I escaped from Alan's house after they killed someone inside. I saw them do it. The Eric you're accusing me of murdering. They had me tied up while they were doing it. And they had the girl, Melody, Melody Anderson, tied up too. They let me go, but they kept her there. I'm telling you the truth. They wouldn't let her go. The rest I found out in the newspapers, on Sunday afternoon. When I read about the car accident. But it was no accident. They did that too. They staged it and caused the car to go into the tree and explode, with Eric's dead body in it, and Melody alive."

"Nice story. Why didn't you go to the police with it. You say you witnessed a murder."

"A murder-accident."

"Why didn't you go to the police immediately, especially, as you tell it, they held a hostage who was in danger?"

"I don't know why. I was scared. I was going to go today.

I was going to go tell the police today."

"Yeah, that's what they all say."

"They, Alan and his friends said they were going to frame me for this. I was trying to see what they had at their house."

"What do you mean frame? Would you like to tell us."

"No, I don't want to say anything else until I have a lawyer."

"Well, I guess that's your right."

"May I have my one phone call now?"

"Yeah, I guess so. Shall we let him make his call?"

"You have to let me make that call!"

"I have one more question I want to ask you. Then you can make your call. What was the nature of your relationship to the young man, Eric Berman"

"None, there was no relationship. He was Alan Prescott's friend."

"Let's just stick to the questions we ask, O.K. Now what was your relationship to Eric Berman. How did you know him?"

"I just met him casually in New York, at an event at the Metropolitan Museum. He was with Alan Prescott. I was just introduced to him last week."

"What night was that?"

"I don't remember."

"Try to remember."

"I don't know. Let's see. I think it was . . . I don't know."

"When was the next time you saw him?"

"The next time was at the party, I saw him at the party at Alan's house. It was Saturday night. He was tied up, in a room downstairs, a kind of torture chamber."

"I think he's been reading too many books. A torture chamber at Mr. Prescott's house? That's a good one."

"I never touched him."

"That's not what we were told by three witnesses."

"What! What did they say!"

"They said you and Eric got quite drunk and started fighting. It turned violent, downstairs at Alan's house. You were fighting over the girl, Melody Anderson."

"What? That's an outright lie. I never fought with Eric. Especially not over a girl. He was gay. He was Alan's lover."

"Boy, you'll come up with just about anything to get out of this one, won't you."

"It's the truth."

"Mr. Prescott is married."

"No, that's impossible."

"He's married to an actress, quite a looker, a tall blond lady, a stage actress in New York."

"That's his wife?"

"Then you know her? Alan, his wife Ingrid Prescott, and the butler said they saw you fighting with Eric, over Melody. Then you took the butler's car and the three of you drove off to settle your argument elsewhere, after you and Eric were ordered to leave the house."

241

"There was another man there, Ernest. I don't know his last name."

"We don't know about any Ernest who was there."

"He's a friend of Alan's. He was there. He assaulted Eric and killed him, assaulted him sexually while he was chained up downstairs."

"They said only you, Mr. Prescott, his wife, Eric and the girl were there at the time of the fight. The butler was called and he threw you out, you, Eric and the girl. By that time, all of the other guests had left."

"They're all lying."

"The butler said he tried to stop you from taking his car, but you sped off too fast down the road."

"I'm telling you the man Ernest was there. He killed Eric. Then they staged the accident to get rid of Eric's body and Melody. She was the only other witness besides me who knew what really happened to Eric. They got rid of her."

"Let's start at the beginning, when you got to the party."

"They said they'd frame me. I need a lawyer."

"I don't think a lawyer's going to help you out of this one, buddy. I've seen some pretty tight cases and this is definitely one of them."

"I have an alibi."

"Hey, he says he has an alibi."

"O.K., I was at the party, but I got back to Sybil's house by 3:00 A.M."

"Did anyone see you?"

"Yes, the maid, Maria, a Spanish woman. She saw me upstairs in the house at 3:00 A.M."

"It doesn't look good for you. You just admitted you didn't get back until 3:00 A.M. Eric Brennan was murdered prior to 3:00 A.M. So you were out and about at the time Eric Brennan was murdered."

"I told you I was there. I told you I saw the man Ernest do it."

"You're a sick man, Mr. Connell, a very sick man. You used the car crash to cover up Eric Brennan's murder, didn't you? And to get rid of the witness, Melody Anderson."

"No, that's a lie. I wasn't there at the time of the crash. I was at Sybil's house."

"What did you use to kill Eric Brennan with?"

"Why don't you tell me, since you know so much about it."

"A knife, you bastard, you used a knife."

"A knife?"

"Write that down. He admits he used a knife. The sick bastard."

"I didn't say that. I didn't say I used a knife."

"I got it right here. You said a knife."

"I was asking you."

"No, you were telling me. He died of knife wounds, not in the car crash."

"No, that's not how he died."

"That's what the autopsy showed."

"That's impossible. I'm not saying another thing. I want a lawyer. I need to make that phone call."

"Where did you hide the murder weapon?"

"I'm not saying. I'm not saying another thing."

"He says he's not going to tell us where he hid the murder weapon. Did you throw it out of the car?"

"No."

"By the side of the road?"

"The side of the road, the side of the road?"

"He says he threw it out of the car. He says it's somewhere by the side of the road."

"What the hell are you talking about. I told you I wasn't in that car. I'm not saying another word. I want my call. I'm entitled to one call."

"What do you say, Jack. Shall we let him make his call. He's doing so good."

"Yeah, go ahead. We've pushed him as far as we can for one night."

"O.K., smart guy, you can make your call now."

"Too bad they don't have the death penalty in New York. That poor young girl, too."

"He'd definitely get that for what he's done."

"Just one more thing. Did you have sexual relations with the girl, Melody Anderson, that night, at Alan Prescott's house? If you cooperate, it usually goes just a bit better for you."

Michael sat silent.

"I'll repeat the question one more time, did you have sexual relations with Melody Anderson the night of the murders?

"Yes."

"Good. The autopsy showed she had fresh semen in her. Her parents said she was a virgin. The lab'll take care of that. Probably raped her, then killed her too."

"Let's see, grand theft auto, rape and murder, two murders. That's all we need to know right now."

"You can make your call now, scumbag."

I dialed the house. "Maria!"

"Oh, Seignor. Are you all right?"

"No. Is Sybil back yet?"

"No, she's not here."

"Shit. Did you try to call her?"

"Yes, Seignor, I did."

"Well, did you reach her?" Did you tell her what's happening, that I've been arrested?"

"No, I couldn't reach here. But I left a message for her to call the house."

"Shit. Did you leave her the message what this is about?"

"No."

"Shit. Well, you better tell her I'm here in jail, in East Hampton. I'm being booked on murder charges. Tell her to come down here immediately. Tell her to get me a lawyer, and it better be a damn good lawyer. It looks like I'm going to need one."

"I weel tell her."

"Your times' up, buddy, hang up the phone."

"O.K. Maria, I'm counting on you. Call her again.'

"I said hang up the phone."

The big fat cop grabbed the phone and slammed Michael against the wall.

"Don't try any funny stuff, 'cause I'd really like to bust you wide open, put my fist through your face, you animal. She must have been pretty, before you burned her to a crisp."

"Come on Jack, get a hold of yourself. You know you can't get away with that crap anymore."

"Just let me get in one good one."

"C'mon Jack, that's enough."

They walked Michael down the long corridor to a cell and the big iron door clanged shut.

Michael just sat there on the cot with a dazed look on his face.

I was ruined. Alan had made good on his promise to frame me. I should have gone to the police right away. I shouldn't have waited. I should have gone there first before Alan had a chance to spin his lies. Shit, it was Monday. Monday night. Exactly one week after I met Sybil at that club in Manhattan. If only I'd stayed home, stayed out at my uncle's farm in Missouri and helped out like he asked me to. If only I hadn't gone up to that bar and met Sybil, if only I hadn't called Melody and gone to Alan's party that night, if only . . . Then I wouldn't be here in this fucking jail cell, with my head about to be lopped off. How the hell am I going to get out of this.? And everyone's on Alan's side, just like he said they would. They don't even question anything he said.

Then the guard came to get me, to take me out to Riverhead Correctional Facility, which is where I'm stuck now.

"Sybil's got to come through for me. Someone's got to believe me."

Herman listened to my story and offered me a smoke, a Camel. It was a little strong, but it seemed to calm my nerves down.

"Seems like you're going to have trouble with that confession they got out of you. Did you sign it?"

"I don't know. After keeping me up all night, I don't know what I signed."

The guard came clicking his shoes down the corridor.

"Visitor for Michael Connell."

After handcuffing me through the bars, he opened my cell. I followed him to the visitor's room. I thought it was the lawyer with more bad news.

I couldn't believe my eyes as I entered the small room. It was Sybil!

"Sybil, I can't believe you're here. You didn't have to come. You shouldn't have come here."

"I heard about it, all of it. I'm sorry, I should have come sooner."

"It's all right. You're here now."

"Maria told me how they took you from the house."

"I never thought you'd come. I thought you'd never want to see me again."

"No Michael, we were filming late yesterday. Maria didn't reach me until it was too late to come and I was exhausted after the long day of shooting. And, well, I had to think about it. The whole thing has been a big shock to me, you getting arrested. Well, I don't think it adds up."

"You mean you believe me, that I didn't kill those two . . . Eric and Melody?"

"Yes."

"Sybil." I tried my best to control my emotions, "I knew you'd come to help me."

"Yes Michael, I'm going to help you. I decided not to let you face this by yourself."

"Sybil, I don't know what to say. I should have never left that night, Saturday night."

"Let's not talk about that right now."

"No, of course not. I swear I'll never betray you again. Never. If you still want me after all this."

"Michael, I let myself in for it. I know I shouldn't have, but I can't stop thinking about you, and right now I've got to help you. I'm going to make sure you have the best damn lawyer that money can buy."

"They've assigned me a public defender, and I don't think he believes one damn thing I told him so far."

"The best criminal defense lawyers usually have a full case load. It might take some time. In the meantime, you better use him. You have to have someone representing you in case they try to question you again. You should have never spoken to the police without a lawyer."

"They twisted everything around. I swear I didn't make that confession."

"Yes, I heard about it and it could be a problem."

"They made it sound like a confession. I couldn't think straight by then."

"Remember, don't talk to them again until I find you a lawyer. In the meantime, you've got to keep the court appointed one. They probably won't let you fire him anyways until a new attorney puts in his appearance.

"O.K., Sybil, whatever you say."

"Michael, I'll make sure he hires the best private investigator to see what he can find out."

"I was there. They removed everything that would incriminate them."

"There must be some slip up somewhere."

"The police think they have a pretty tight case against me, on both murders."

"Well at least we know you were back to my house at the time they say the car crash took place. I'll make Maria testify to that."

"What about Alan? Won't he try to ruin your career if you go against him?

"He's already threatened. He said if I did anything to help you, he'd ruin me, professionally, financially, in any way he could. And that I'd never work in Hollywood again."

"Can he do that?"

"He's going to try."

"Sybil,! You're still going to do this for me?"

"He's not the only power that's out there, although he's very important. There are other people, other studios, and the independent companies that back films."

"Sybil, you're really going to risk everything to do this for me?"

"I have to do what's right. I'm not going to be controlled by anyone and especially not on anything as serious as this."

"I don't know what to say."

The guard came to get Sybil, "Time's up. Time to leave Miss."

"He's not going to try to stop the filming, is he?"

"I don't know. I think he's going to try."

"Oh shit, how's he going to do that? Isn't it already funded?"

Sybil stood up to leave, "We're over budget and behind schedule. He's going to try to take over the picture from me. Have me replaced with another producer."

"Well, you better get out here right now."

The guard waited impatiently.

"I'll make some calls later, when we take a break. I'll find you that lawyer, don't worry."

The guard escorted Sybil out.

That was great, just what I was hoping for all along, that Sybil would come through and not abandon me altogether. I really was falling in love with her, totally and helplessly in love. It was real this time. I don't think I ever even knew what love was. To stay with someone, to be loyal to them, no matter what, no matter what they did. To forgive them.

The guard led me back to my cell. Herman was already eating lunch, which turned out to be a real lethal concoction, not exactly what I was used to at Sybil's. I wasn't even sure what it was, something grey and oozy. Just as I was about to doze off, trying to feel better now that I knew Sybil was behind me, the guard shows up. The court appointed lawyer was waiting to see me. I was taken to the visitor's room. Mr. Kapp was silent for a moment.

"Well, what is it?"

"It's not shaping up too good for you. Remember when they brought you in, they searched the house."

"But if they didn't have a search warrant, they can't use any of that as evidence, right?"

"Oh, they had a search warrant all right. It was all nice and legal. They searched your room and found some very incriminating evidence."

"Oh yeah and what was that."

"They found Eric's clothes in your room. Actually they found them in your suitcase in the closet. That was bad enough, but then they ran a lab test on them and found traces of Eric's hair and blood on the shirt. What were they doing in your closet?"

"Shit, I kept meaning to get rid of those clothes, but I never got the chance. Then the police showed up."

"Not good."

"Look, I can explain those clothes. Alan gave me those clothes. Mine were all ripped up, cut up by Alan after he chained me to the wall in his basement. When they decided to let me go, he just picked up some clothes off the floor and gave them to me."

"That's not what they said."

"They?"

"Alan, his wife and his butler. No, it's not looking too good for you. And they found one of your shoes in the trunk of that car, the car you said you never entered. They found the match to it in your closet, one brown Armani loafer."

"Shit, the shoe."

"It was half burned up, but they knew it was yours by the match to it in your closet.'

"Shit, they put that shoe in the car. I told you they said they would try to frame me."

"Michael, let's face it, it's not looking good for you or your version of the story."

"It's not a story, its all true."

"Why didn't you tell me about the shoe, or Eric's clothes?"

"I forgot. I thought it wasn't important."

"I told you, everything is important. If you're not being truthful with me, how do you expect me to help you? You're making my job really hard, and believe me, it's hard enough already."

"The dogs got my shoe, when I was escaping over the gate."

"I thought you said they let you go."

"The dogs were loose. They almost bit my foot off, but they got the shoe instead. Alan must have found it and put it in the trunk of that Buick."

"What about the clothes?"

"I told you, they gave me those clothes, so I could leave the house."

"Why did they let you go? According to your story, you witnessed a murder. Why did they just let you go and not the girl?"

"I don't know. They thought I wouldn't talk."

"Why did they think that?"

"Because they had my fucking fingerprints all over everything."

"Now you tell me all this. You should have told me everything this morning, especially in a case like this. Everything is critical and time is ticking down against you. Don't you think I want to win this case for you?"

"No."

"That's great. You've got to have some faith in your own lawyer."

"Alright. I suppose you're all I got right now. Sybil could change her mind and not hire another lawyer, or let Alan get to her. But I think she's going to come through for me after all."

"Come on Michael, we're just wasting valuable time. I've got lots of other cases, you know, some just as serious as yours. Is there anything else you'd like to tell me about now?"

"No!"

"Michael, with all this evidence piling up against you, everything they come up with is confirming the police report of the events. And then there's the confession. I think you ought to cooperate, or at least consider a plea bargain. Plead guilty to second degree murder, with extenuating circumstances. It'll really cut down your time."

"I'm not pleading guilty to anything."

"No, I didn't say to do it, I just said to consider it. I can talk to the prosecutor and see what he's willing to offer, see what we can work out. I know he really wants to try your case. It'll bring lots of publicity for him. He's got ambition. He wants to run for District Attorney for the State of New York. Well, I don't know if you're aware of it, but it's a pretty sensational case. It's all over the newspapers."

"Yeah, I know."

"And the way they're portraying you, it's looking pretty bad."

"O.K., O.K., just see what he's offering. I'm not agreeing to anything. Just see."

"Good choice. I'll see what he says and I'll get back to you. Wise decision."

"I said I'm not agreeing to anything right now."

"In the meantime, see if you can think of anything else, anything that might help you."

"Yeah, I'll wrack my brains out the whole time you're gone."

The lawyer picked up his briefcase and called for the guard to let him out.

When I was returned to my cell, I told Herman what the lawyer said.

"Yeah, see what I told you. That's what they all do, those public defenders. They try to get you to agree to a plea bargain so you'll plead guilty and lighten their work load."

"I guess you're right."

"They don't have the time to really try a case."

"But maybe Sybil will come through for me and hire that lawyer."

"She better be ready to lay out some very big bucks. Did they offer you bail?"

"Yeah, one million dollars."

"But if they find a bail bondsman, it's only ten percent, just a hundred grand cash, but you've got to have someone put up collateral for the rest. If they consider you a flight risk, then, they got to put up the whole thing."

"I can't ask her to do that. They already said I was a flight risk."

"Go ahead, ask. You'd be surprised what people might do if just ask them."

"How about you? Can't you get out on bail?"

"No, it's my second time through. There is no bail. Bail was refused. You'd think I'd learn the first time, but times are rough. I've got a wife and four kids to feed. We can't live off the $4.50 an hour I was getting."

"Well, you're going to have a harder time feeding them from in here."

"Yeah, well, you're not doing too good yourself from what I heard, with that tight ass lawyer you got."

"I know, I know."

"Here comes the guard again."

"More good news, no doubt." Herman quickly put out his cigarette.

"Michael Connell, your lawyer is here to see you."

Michael sat down in the visitors' room and listened to what Kapp had to say this time. He had a sinking feeling it was not going to be good news.

"Michael, I've got to talk to you. More bad news. I just called the D.A.'s office."

"Well, come on, what did he say."

"They found the murder weapon."

"What? What murder weapon? There was no murder weapon."

"O.K., Michael, they found what they're calling the murder weapon, the knife, the knife you confessed that you used to kill Eric Berman with. They found it by the side of the road, near the car, the blue Buick, just like you said in confession. They're saying you must have thrown it out before you ditched the car with the two people in it. Before the car exploded or was set on fire that caused the fuel tank to explode. That's what they're saying now."

"I told you there was no knife."

"Well, this knife has your fingerprints all over it. They just got it back from the lab."

"What? What does this knife look like?"

"It has a large engraved ornamental top. It's made of silver."

"What, in silver? I never saw a knife. I never touched a knife at Alan's house. Wait a minute. How could they do that? There was a silver belt buckle that belonged to Eric, with a piece of turquoise in it. They made me put my fingerprints all over that."

"Well, this knife has a large silver handle that just happened to have a piece of turquoise in it. So you've just described it perfectly."

"Shit, they must have had Eric belt buckle made into the handle for the knife."

"Well, Eric's prints and blood are all over it, too. Looks like you two had quite a struggle over the knife."

"This is ridiculous. I told you there was no struggle. There was no knife."

"Well, there is now and the police have it as evidence."

"Next, I'll probably hear they have a video tape of me fighting with Eric and cutting him with a fatal stab wound. Shit, they're very good at this."

"How could they have a videotape?"

265

"I didn't say they had a videotape. I said they could probably come up with one. Trick photography or something. They're in the movie business, you know."

"They haven't produced any videotape, at least not yet. Michael, I don't have to tell you, but it's looking worse and worse for you and the papers are going nuts over this."

"What's that got to do with it?"

"They don't like you. They're making you out to be some sort of sick psycho. And once the public and the press go against you, well, you're sort of a dead dog."

"I thought I was supposed to be tried in a court of law, not in the streets or by the press."

"Well, that's how it's supposed to work, but we're all human, and no one is immune to bad publicity. And yours is getting worse by the minute."

"What do I have to do, hire a P.R. agent?"

"It wouldn't hurt."

"You've got to be kidding."

"No, unfortunately I'm not."

"So now I have to ask Sybil to pay for a public relations person as well as a lawyer?"

"Oh, you're still trying to get your friend to hire you a private lawyer?"

"Of course. What evidence have you come up with for my side of the story against that gang of liars and murderers?"

"We don't have funds to hire private investigators and experts right now. The police and their labs are the experts, but that's what you need now, a private investigator, if it will do any good, but I seriously doubt it."

"Have you taken the maid's statement, about my returning home at 3:00 A.M., to Sybil's house?"

"No, not yet."

"What are you waiting for, Christmas or the day after I'm found guilty?"

"Now Michael, there's no need to be sarcastic. I don't think that will help anyways."

"Are you going to help me or help them try to hang me?"

"Michael, you must know that our funds are very limited. You've got to help me. Tell me what evidence I should be looking for."

"Blood, blood on the floor at Alan's house, blood on a rug, an oriental rug they wrapped Eric up in, after he lay dying, in the room downstairs. He bled all over that rug. Maybe they didn't have time to get rid of it yet."

"Where should I look?"

"At Alan's house, you idiot. I've been explaining all this to you all along."

"The police were in that room, and there was no torture chamber, just a storage room with lots of furniture in it."

"Just get out to Alan's house and look around. Try to find Eric's blood on the floor of that room, try to find that carpet. That would prove they're all lying. 'Cause that's where they killed him. Not after he left the house. Before he left the house. They removed his body after they killed him.

"Well, at least you're being consistent."

"I told you what really happened, you moron."

"I can't work with you if you keep insulting me. They'll have to find you someone else."

"Shit, are you going to defend me or not?"

"Michael, do you want my honest opinion?"

"Here we go again."

"I really think you should strike a plea bargain with the D.A. before you go to trial. At this point, a trial doesn't look too good for you. All the evidence is stacking up against you. Even if I can get them to throw out that confession, which won't be easy. It has your signature on it."

"I didn't know what I was signing."

"I can say it was a forced confession, that they confused you. But then there's still all that evidence."

"Circumstantial."

"And the testimony of three people."

"Liars and murderers."

"Their word against yours."

"What about Sybil's maid?"

"She's the maid of your lover, as I understand it. They'll just think she put the maid up to give you an alibi, to cover you at the time of the car crash. Not exactly a neutral party. Plus the alibi doesn't cover the time of Eric's death, which is put at least one hour before the wreck, which would give you plenty of time to get back to your lover's house."

"So that's how it is."

"Yes, I"m afraid so. Look, I'm trying to be straightforward with you, Michael. There's no sense me making it out to be better than it is. I would be doing a great disservice to you, as your attorney."

"Yeah, I guess you're right."

"So I can go to the D.A. and ask for a shorter sentence, about twenty years, with a few you can get off for good behavior. At least you'll know what you're dealing with."

A look of incredulity came over Michael's face.

"What, are you fucking kidding me? Please guilty to murder?" Get twenty years? I'll be fucking forty-five by the time I get out, all for a crime I didn't commit."

"It's your choice, Michael, a twenty with time off for good behavior, or pretty near a sure thing a life sentence if the judge throws the book at you, and he might for double homicide. What with the public outcry out here on Long Island, you might get life with no possibility of parole. Those are the facts, Michael, and you'd better think long and hard about this You could die an old man behind bars without a plea bargain."

"Hey dirt bag, I was told about you public defenders."

"You don't need to call me any more names. These are the facts as I see them, and I'm just doing my job. I'm trying to defend you."

"If you were trying to defend me you'd be out trying to get the evidence against them. The three of them did it, Alan, Ernest and Alan's wife Ingrid."

271

"O.K., wise guy, by those three you mean Alan, Ingrid Prescott, and the butler, right? Their stories are all identical. They were each asked separately, but their stories match up exactly. I've seen the transcript. There is no Ernest. Who is he? Nobody knows about any Ernest."

"Ernest was the one who killed Eric, probably accidentally. He's a middle aged man, dark hair, with a stocky build. Alan admitted to me when I was at his house that Ernest took a ticket under Alan's name Monday morning and flew out to L.A. When the police showed up at Alan's house, he had the butler tell them he had left for L.A., but he was still there. Alan was just avoiding being interrogated by the police and having his house searched. He needed time for them all to get their story straight and have the house professionally swept of evidence. You see, they fabricated this whole thing against me. I was their only witness, at least the only one who lived, and that's why they didn't kill me. I see it now. They needed a fall guy to take the blame for the double murder. Don't you see? It all fits together now. I'm their scapegoat."

"I don't really see anything, except everything points directly to you."

"That's what I mean, they set it up perfectly to all fall on me. That's why they let me go and not Melody."

"Well, Michael, you better really think about what I told you and what I can ask the prosecutor for. There's no guarantee he's even going to agree to it, but I think I can convince him. It will be a victory for him, a conviction without costing the taxpayers all that money for a lengthy trial. Yeah, that's exactly how I'll present it to him, so he can think he'll still look good for his campaign."

"I don't give a damn about his campaign."

"Oh, but he does, believe me."

"You think you're going to sell me down the road for twenty years. Why don't you try twenty years yourself if you think it's so fucking light. I'm innocent, you bastard."

"Michael, you better think about it. I got to get going. "

"Yeah, you better get going before I strangle you, you son of a bitch."

Kapp looked at Michael's manacled wrists and then up at Michael. "Yeah, well I'll see you tomorrow before you have to plead in front of the judge. Let's see if you change your mind by then."

The attorney left quickly, looking behind him at Michael as he was taken out by the guard of visitor's room.

When Michael was returned to his cell, it was already dinner time.

Herman put out his Camel. "Pretty bad, huh?"

"Yeah,"

I wouldn't want to be in your shoes. At least I'm not accused of killing anyone."

"Yeah." Michael was in a daze. He didn't know what to do. Maybe the lawyer was right. He was starting to lose all hope. Maybe Sybil wouldn't get that high priced lawyer after all. He felt the walls closing in around him.

"I'll be out in a few years, with time off for good behavior. I'm definitely planning to go straight this time. My family's been through enough, but I do have a parole hearing coming up in a just a few months. Maybe I'll make it this time."

"He wants me to plead guilty, but I didn't even do anything. I didn't kill anyone."

"Well don't let him talk you into anything. Once you sign that form, that's it, it's all over. You can't change your mind after that. The plea bargain. Then you're signed, sealed and delivered for the term. No appeals."

"I'll never accept that."

"That's right. You hang tough. Don't let him bullshit you. That's what he wants and then he can move on to his next case. Who knows, maybe you could still pull that rabbit out of the hat. It's been done before."

"It has?"

"Yes, a jury's a very unpredictable thing."

"You really think I have a chance?"

"Sure. There was the Claus Von Bulow case in Newport, Rhode Island. I saw the movie. The fucker probably did his wife in with an overdose of insulin in a needle they found in a bag. During the first trial, he got really bad publicity. Then, for some reason, I forget what, he had a second trial on the same charges, to see if he was guilty of murdering his wife who had a huge fortune and one those famous mansions in Newport.

"What happened at the second trial?"

"He hired the best team of publicity agents money could buy. You'd think he was running for office, they put on such a huge media campaign. And guess what? They redid his image from the evil conniving villain to a nice humorous, fun loving guy. He hired the best lawyers money could buy."

"So, what happened?"

"He got off scott free."

"He did?"

"Yeah, he got to keep all his wife's money and property, the mansion in Newport, the apartment on Park Avenue, everything."

"That's terrible."

"Then he remarried and moved back to Europe. That's where he's from."

"Do you think he really did it?"

"Of course, he's guilty as sin. There was a pile of evidence against him, but that's the power of money for you."

"That's terrible."

"Well, that's life. You hire the best, you get off. That's America for you. That's how white folks get away with murdering and robbing people. Just let my sorry ass try that."

"Well, thanks for the encouragement, that is if Sybil comes through for me. I guess she's my only hope now. She said she would, but she could change her mind."

"Stop torturing yourself, man, she told you she would. Once she gets the loot out and hires the best guns, you're worries are almost over."

"You really think so?"

"Sure."

"But I'm up against a really powerful and wealthy man."

"Well of course that makes it more difficult, but not impossible."

"I guess you're right, Herman."

"It just depends on how good a lawyer you get. It has nothing to do with the truth."

"Thanks Herman for your talk. I sure needed that right now."

"And don't be thinking about doing anything stupid again. I've got my eye on you, a young dude like you with your whole life ahead of you."

"Don't worry. You know I was thinking about ending it rather than spend the rest of my life like a rat in a cage, but not noe. I thought I was never going to get out."

"Shit, this ain't nothing. At least you can keep breathing... and have a smoke once in awhile." Herman took a long drag on his Camel.

"I thought I was alone and that it was all over. I'm from Missouri, you know. I've only been here a few weeks. "

The guard came and announced, "A phone call for Michael Connell. You can take it over here."

"Hello. Sybil? I'm so glad to hear your voice. It doesn't look good. What, you can't make it back here today? What about the lawyer? "

Michael let out a big sigh of relief, "That's great. It's what I was hoping for. The best? That'll sure help me sleep better tonight. Yes, I was worried, with that goon of a public defender. No, I won't listen to him. When he is coming to see me? . . . Tomorrow? That's great Sybil. How can I repay you? Ha ha, yeah, you'll think of something. What, a bail bond? No Sybil, don't even think of it. O.K. I'll see you tomorrow. "

"You sure are lucky to know someone like that."

"Yeah, I know."

"Don't blow it."

"No, I won't blow it this time, Herman. No way."

"Well, we all have our lessons to learn. That's what it's all about. I know. I learned to curb my wicked ways with women and now a got a real good woman who stands by her man, even a bank robber. She's waiting for me to get out."

"That's great. Goodnight Herman, I can't stay awake any longer. It's been an exhausting day."

CHAPTER 15 - Wednesday, August 6
Riverhead Correctional Facility

Right after breakfast, Sybil came through for me, true to her word. The famous criminal lawyer Dan Murphy came to see me, lil ol' me, Michael Connell. I'd read about him lots of times with his high profile cases. And nine out of ten times he won. I just hoped I wouldn't be his tenth case.

When Herman heard he was waiting for me in the visitor's room, he gave me a high five and said I was as good as free. I couldn't get to the visitor's room fast enough.

"Michael, my name is Dan Murphy and I've been hired to defend you. I don't have to tell you, you face very serious charges. They're thinking of upgrading it to double murder, especially after they heard I was taking the case.

"That's great."

"They've just finished gathering more evidence and the

prosecutor is looking it over. They're going to try to pin the girl's murder on you too."

"I knew that was coming."

"And I also have to tell you, the evidence together with the statements of those three people, Alan Prescott, his wife Ingrid and their butler Stanley, all point directly to you as the only suspect."

"Great."

"That's the bad part. The good part is I'm working on getting your so-called confession wiped out, as coercion.

"It's about time."

"It looks like the police twisted your words around pretty good. The public defender was working on getting the prosecutor to drop the first homicide to second degree, but with the rape and murder of the girl, they're calling that one premeditated. So we've got our work cut out for us."

"You mean I'm in a worse position now?"

"No, it means you're going to have to fully cooperate with me and don't hide anything, even things that don't make you out to be a hero, or details you don't think are important. If you do that, then I think we have a fighting chance."

"You do? You think we really have a chance of winning?"

"Hey, I didn't get my reputation by only taking the easy cases. Usually, at the beginning, they all look as bad as yours, or even worse. But when I start looking into them, looking under the surface for things that aren't easily apparent, that's when I get the case to start to turn around. That's when I start to earn my fee, which some consider a king's ransom. But somehow I manage to find those little details that decide if a man goes to the electric chair or not. Of course there's no death penalty here in New York, so you don't have to worry about that."

"There are several things, but the court appointed attorney, Attorney Kapp, couldn't be bothered to find them."

"Forget about him. We let him go this morning."

"What a relief."

"He was ready to send you down stream for about twenty years. He and the prosecutor had it all worked out."

"I know."

"You're a very lucky young man. Your friend Sybil is determined to do everything she can for you. As a matter of fact, I think she's pledging her house right now as collateral for the bail."

"No, you're kidding."

"No, I'm not. Earlier this morning I went in front of the judge to try to get your bail reduced in half to $500,000.00, but the judge refused. He said you're a high flight risk. The bondsman insisted on getting $100,000.00 cash and collateralizing the rest, secured by Sybil's house for $900,000.00. So you better not be thinking of taking any trips or there goes Sybil's lovely East Hampton beach house."

"No, I'm not going anywhere. I want to see the right people come to justice for what they did."

"Well, that's not my job. I'm only here to get you out of this. That's all. I'll be up to the prosecutor to see if he wants to pursue other avenues after we've presented all of our evidence."

"I guess I'll have to accept that for now."

"When do I get out of here?"

"Later today, sometime this afternoon after all the paperwork is processed.'

"That's fantastic. I can hardly believe it's true."

"I'm just doing my job. And don't forget, I don't like to lose."

"Well I hope your luck keeps up on this one."

"Luck has nothing to do with it. Being absolutely thorough, hiring the best investigators, and I forgot to tell you, I'm playing golf with the D.A. this afternoon, at the Maidstone Club. I'm the token black member they let join."

"You're seeing the D.A.?"

"Yes. I've read all the transcripts. So we don't need to repeat that. I have everything you told Kapp about the night of the murder of Eric Brennan. But think, take your time, try to think of anything else that will help me defend you, anything that will help me refute the case they're building against you. I hate to say it, but their case looks pretty solid right now. We've got to come up with something pretty good or all the golf dates in the world aren't going to help you."

"O.K. This is what I've been trying to tell Kapp since yesterday. There is evidence to collect that could help me, but he wouldn't do anything about it."

"Shit. That evidence needed to be collected immediately before it's altered or removed. This isn't a good start."

"There was no fight between Eric and me at Alan's house. The man named Ernest did it while Eric was chained to the wall in a soundproof room on the lower level. That's where Eric bled to death. But now, they have it looking like a storage room."

"O.K., we'll get right on it. Better late than never."

"He bled a lot, poor guy after Ernest viciously sexually assaulted him. But maybe some of the blood seeped through between the floor boards into the wood. Then they wrapped him up in a large oriental rug, and the poor guy bled all over that. If you can find that rug..."

"Good. I'm getting an investigator on this the minute I get out of here. Maybe it's not too late. I'm sure they think they have this all sewed up now that you're put away in here."

"You're probably right. Alan seemed pretty relaxed when I found him in his projection room Monday morning."

"What! You were over there and you saw Alan Prescott?"

"Yes."

"Wasn't he supposed to be in L.A.? The police were trying to ask him some questions and search his house Monday morning, but according to the police report, they couldn't gain access."

"He was there alright. I went back Monday morning to try to find the stuff they were using to frame me like Eric's belt buckle that they turned into the top of the knife."

"You shouldn't have gone there."

"We got into a fight and I punched him a few times, but I couldn't find anything there. They had me put my fingerprints on Eric's belt buckle and on Eric's Ray Ban sunglasses the night of the murder. I guess they didn't need the sunglasses because they haven't turned up yet."

"I see. That explains your fingerprints on the knife."

"My fingerprints were on the bottle of Johnny Walker Red they found near the burned out Buick."

"I guess they haven't tested that bottle yet. Tell me about Ernest. He's not mentioned in any part of the police report."

"He was there. He's the one that killed Eric. He's the one who took Alan's plane ticket and flew to L.A. Monday morning."

"We'll see what we can come up with about him. Now think, Michael, is there anything else?"

"No, not really. Except Alan admitted to following the Buick that Eric's body and Melody were in. I think she was still alive at the time. Those bastards burned her to death. Wait, the photograph of the scene in the newspaper showed a white scarf on the ground. She wore a white scarf on the night of the party, and I'm sure she must have thrown it out the window before the car exploded."

"I'll have all his vehicles checked, inside and out. Anything else?"

"Yes, when I left the property, or rather after Alan let me out the side door Saturday night, I had Eric's clothes on. Alan had cut mine off me and I was handed Eric's clothes to wear which were crumpled up on the floor. But his dogs were loose and I was chased by two of them to the rear gate. His dog got a hold of one of my loafers as I was trying to climb over the gate. This is the Armani loafer they found in the trunk of the Buick. They found the other one in my closet at Sybil's."

"This is not good, Michael. Anything else?"

"Yes, the dogs made quite a racket and woke a neighbor who lived across the road from the back gate. He spotted me cutting across his lawn and he came out with a rifle and said something about blowing my head of if I came back to rob his house again."

"Excellent. This is excellent Michael. This is just the sort of stuff we need to corroborate your version of the events."

"Thanks, Dan. Can I call you Dan?"

"Yes, please do."

"Well Dan, it's a lot easier to think when you're talking to someone who's really on your side, someone who believes in what you're saying."

"That's what I'm paid to do."

"Dan, I wasn't exactly looking forward to spending twenty years in prison for a crime I didn't commit."

"It doesn't happen that often, but once is too much, to send an innocent man to prison. This stuff you just told me is very important. What about the morning after the murders up to the time you were arrested. They say she died in the car you were supposed to be driving very early Sunday morning when you left Alan's house with Eric and Melody. The witnesses say Eric and Melody were alive when you drove away from Alan's house."

"They're all lies!"

"I know, I know, just be sure to tell me everything about early Sunday Morning."

"After I ran back from Alan's house Saturday night, I entered through the window to my room on the second floor, the same way I left. I tiptoed to Sybil's room down the hallway to see her, but she was asleep. I felt nauseous and dizzy so I turned around and went back to my bedroom and fell asleep, exhausted. I think I just passed out."

"Of course we'll do everything that's in my power, everything possible." Dan stood up to leave and shook my hand even though I was still had handcuffs on in front of me.

"Well, I better get going. I've got a lot to do, but you gave me some good leads. I'll put an investigator on this right away. We'll use an independent lab to analyze anything we find. They don't even know what they're looking for, and they don't seem to care. The police think they have a water tight case In their minds, they have their man and that's all the prosecutor needs. It's up to us to prove you're innocent. "

Dan looked at his watch. "Uh oh, I better get out of here. Can't be late for my tee time with the D.A. You'd be surprised how important those golf games can be."

Dan winked at me through his horn rimmed designer glasses. He was a tall, straight-backed man in an expensive dark grey pinstripe suit, a perfectly starched white shirt and a silk tie with golfers swinging their clubs on it. He looked expensive and he looked beyond confident, like he didn't have a care in the world. I liked that and it made me want to relax, but I couldn't.

I couldn't get rid of the feeling of impending doom until the whole thing was over, if it was ever going to be over. But at least now I had a fighting chance.

As the guard let him out, Dan turned and said, "By the way, Sybil said she'd send for you as soon as the bail is taken care of. Enjoy your last hours of prison life." Dan it seemed had a weird sense of humor.

I was led back to the cell and told Herman about the meeting with the great man, Dan Murphy.

"See, what'd I tell you. Money talks and bullshit walks. Feature that, you got yourself an expensive black lawyer."

"Sybil said he's the best around, a Yale law school graduate, and he seems to really care about what he's doing. Thanks for holding my hand during my darkest hours. I won't forget you Herman."

"Now don't you go telling nobody that, homey, that Herman held a white boy's hand, 'cause they're going to be calling me all sorts of names and it could ruin my reputation."

"I won't forget you Herman, I mean it."

"Yes, you will, the minute your white ass walks through those gates, you're going to forget all about ol' Herman."

"The first thing I'm going to do is stop at the commissary and get you a carton of cigarettes, Camels."

"I'll see it when I believe it. You can't get me any pot, can you?"

"I think I'm in enough trouble as it is."

"That stuff is really expensive in here, but it calms my nerves. I don't want anything to go wrong before I come up for parole. Shit, if they gave it to dudes in here, they'd be a lot mellower and there'd be a lot less fighting going on."

The guard came and called my name, "Michael Connell. You've been bailed out. We're escorting you for processing right now."

"Man that was fast. Your lawyer sure is quick, dude. Good luck. I hope you do get off man, I really do."

"Thanks Herman, thanks for everything. I won't forget you. They'll be sending up that carton pretty soon."

"Good, I'm just about to run out. Take care of yourself."

I couldn't believe it. I was actually walking out of here, out of this place when I was thinking of taking my life yesterday. Was it only yesterday? It seems like weeks, months, years ago. I can't believe it was only yesterday. I pictured my body hanging there in the cell and I thought I saw Melody, with that sweet smile of hers walking towards me down a long eerily lit corridor. She looked so angelic. She turned around and beckoned me to follow her. Then I saw she was walking on clouds, she was in heaven.

I snapped out it and thought no, I'm not ready to join her yet. The priest who visited me earlier in the day said it was a sin to try to take your own life. He said only the Lord knows when it's your time to go from your earthly bounds. And look at me now, walking out of here. It would have been a terrible mistake, one I wouldn't have been able to undo. And now everything's changed and it's only one day later.

The guard at the desk signed me out, gave me back the clothes I came in with, all Ralph Lauren, the envelope with my Gucci watch, the gold jewelry Sybil had bought me at Fortunoff's, and my dollar seventy-five. Then I was led to the outside gate. As I approached the black limo I saw Cecil smiling at me through the window.

"Welcome back, Michael."

"I see you're back from your trip."

As I approached the limo, I was surprised to see Sybil sitting in the back seat.

"Sybil, what are you doing here?" Aren't you supposed to be filming?"

"Michael, I didn't want to tell you, but Alan closed down the film this morning."

"No!"

"Yes, as soon as he heard I was hiring Dan Murphy to defend you. But don't worry about it. I'll get back at him. Somehow."

"We'll both get him.

I was so happy to see Sybil. I sat pressed up against her and kissed her with so much passion, a passion I never felt before. I kissed her again, so long, so deep, it took my breath away. It was just like the first night we met, in the back seat, making mad passionate love when we drove through the streets of New York. No, it wasn't like the night I met her at the Red Zone, that whacked out bar. This was different, totally different. I pushed the button putting up the window that separated us from Cecil, but this time she didn't stop me. Then I made love to her, but it felt like real love, not just sex. It was the hottest sex I'd ever had in my life. I just tore her clothes off. I couldn't stop. Our souls seemed joined together now, not just our bodies. I knew now we were going to be together for a very long time, at least if I had anything to do with it, and, of course, if Dan got me off. I just learned a hard lesson, what loyalty meant. Sticking by a person no matter what they did, no matter how difficult it was, and Sybil certainly did that for me. Nobody had ever done anything like that for me before. She came through for me in spite of what I had done.

I never experienced anything like that before. It was better than any drug, better than anything, really. It was a feeling that just kept going on and on, and I just came, coming and coming again as she held me tightly, and we came together I don't know how many times. Yes, it was definitely better than any drug, and you didn't need a refill. We only each other. We looked into each other's eyes and held one another tight. I never wanted to let her go.

I had finally found home and it was Sybil.

It wasn't a house, it wasn't a room, it wasn't a place. I never knew that. Home was finally finding that other person and then you could be anywhere, anywhere on the face of the earth, and you would be home. Yes, I was in love. Finally, I knew what love was, totally, truly. I was in fact addicted to Sybil. I had to have her day and night, and all day long. I absolutely had to have her all the time.

"Sybil, I don't know what to say. I hope Alan hasn't ruined your career. He ruined the picture you poured so much into. I feel terribly guilty and responsible. What a horrible waste."

"Don't worry. I'll overcome all that. I'll bounce right back because there's one thing he can't take away me, my talent and my dedication as a producer."

"But I feel responsible for all that, the cause of it all. I have to make it up to you, somehow."

I was determined to. If only the trial was behind me, and if Dan Murphy was able to prove me innocent. He just had to. We made love all the way back to Sybil's house, and even when we started up the driveway, I didn't want to let her go.

CHAPTER 16 - Wednesday, August 6, East Hampton

When we pulled up in front of Sybil's house, the house seemed different. The house was now pledged to the bail bondsman and that seemed to take away some of its magic, like it didn't really belong to her anymore. I went straight to my room to take a long hot shower, to wash out the sounds and smells of that place and what it did to me. I wanted to burn it out of my system with the hot steaming water. I gave myself a shave, splashing on lots of Sybil's favorite aftershave, Safari. Once I was dressed in some fresh clothes, Ralph Lauren jeans and a blue and white striped Lauren shirt, I almost felt like a new man. I say almost, because in the back of my mind, I knew I still had Murder One hanging over me.

The bell rang. I rushed downstairs, reliving the nightmare of the police coming to get me just a few short days ago. But it wasn't the police. It was a short grey haired man in a trench coat wearing clear framed eyeglasses.

"Are you Michael Connell?" he asked in a scary official tone.

I hesitated, "What do you want?"

"My name is Bernie Gottlieb and Dan Murphy sent me over. I'm a private investigator. He hired me to help with your case."

After I recovered from the fright he gave me, of the deja vue of being handcuffed and stuffed into the back seat of the patrol car, I was able to speak, "In that case, come on in."

I led him to a long white sofa in the glass walled living room, but he stood and said, "I think it would be best if you come with me when I try to find evidence at Alan Prescott's house, since you know where everything should be, where it all took place and exactly where I should look for the stuff. I think we should leave right away." He did take a moment to admire the view of the waves crashing on the beach.

"Yes, you're right. Do you think they're going to just let us walk in there? They didn't even let the police in when I was there. This isn't exactly in their best interests."

"No, I suppose not. Why don't you let me take care of things. That's why I have a court order."

"That Dan's really fast, kind of amazing. I guess that's why they say he's one of the best in the business."

"Yeah, let's get going. You go in my car."

"I'll be right down. I have to tell Sybil."

Bernie looked around at the magnificent view of the ocean and the unusual architecture as he waited, smoking a short fat cigar and dropping ashes on the white carpet.

As we drove to Alan's house, Bernie said, "Look, you know we don't have a lot of time of our side. People forget, people change things in their minds. After we go through Alan's house, and

I hope he isn't home. I don't want a confrontation between you two. Then I'm going to interview that neighbor, the one you said pulled a shotgun on you. I hope he doesn't try to shoot me. Only kidding. I know how to handle these things."

"Bernie, you have a strange sense of humor."

"You have to, to stay sane in this business.'

Bernie's white Chrysler LeBaron convertible, which had seen better days, made its way on the winding roads to Alan's house. He decided to stop at the neighbors first, to get that out of the way. Bernie stood on the man's front porch smoking his cheap cigar, which had an acrid smell to it. He leant on the doorbell with his elbow. Soon, a lady came to the door.

"Hello, how can I help you. You're not one of those horrible salesmen are you?"

Bernie was holding a tattered large black briefcase in one hand.

"No, Ma'am. I'm here as part of a criminal investigation and it's very important I speak with your husband." Bernie handed her an official looking card. "Is he home?"

She looked it over. " Oh, O.K., I'll go get him." She looked flustered as she looked down at the card. It had a Sheriff's insignia on it.

As she went to get her husband, Bernie whispered in Michael's ear, "Honorary Sheriff, you know."

The man came to the door a few minutes later. "What's this all about?" He didn't seem happy.

"I have a few questions to ask you. It's about last Saturday night. It's part of a case I'm investigating. You might be able to help."

"Oh, yeah, that one in the papers. Too bad, those two young people. Yeah, I read about it."

"Do you remember the party across the road that took place last Saturday night?"

"Sure, lots of fancy cars, lots of people. Most left about midnight though. I know 'cause that's about when we went to bed, once the racket of all those cars leaving died down."

"Good. Now did you sleep all through the night 'till morning, or did you get up for something?"

"Yes, as a matter of fact I did, about two hours later. How did you know?"

"Go on."

"It was about two in the morning when I heard all this racket with the neighbor's guard dogs. They're real vicious creatures. "

"Then what happened?"

"I have real sensitive ears. We got robbed here about a week ago. All that summer trash coming down here from the city, so when I heard the dogs causing a ruckus, I looked out the window."

"And what did you see?"

"A guy climbing over the gate over there, and then coming onto my property. So I grabbed my shot gun and I was going do some hunting right here on my front lawn. But he took off before I could get him."

"You say about two A.M.?"

"Yes, that's right, more like 2:30, something like that.

"Did you say anything to him?"

"I don't remember."

"Try to remember. It could be very important to this case."

"O.K., I said something like I was going to blow his head off if I caught him here again, but he took off through the brush and that was the last I saw him."

"Did you get a look at him?"

"No, it was too dark."

"Well, thanks a lot Mr. . . . What did you say your name was?"

"Rooney, Arnold Rooney."

"Thanks, Mr. Rooney, you've been a big help."

"Just doing my duty as a citizen."

"I have been recording what you just said. You don't object to my recording your answers, do you?"

"No."

"Good, then you won't mind signing it once my secretary types it up."

"No, of course not, if it's what I said."

"Thanks very much, Mr. Rooney. We do appreciate your cooperation."

"Not at all. Glad to be of some assistance." Mr. Rooney seemed relieved the interview was over and went inside.

"Today is Wednesday, August 4th and I have just recorded Mr. Arnold Rooney's statement, here at 16 Newton Lane, East Hampton," Bernie spoke into the microphone.

"Onward and upward, Michael," Bernie said as he stamped out his cigar on Mr. Rooney's pristine white gravel driveway.

"What's next? That was pretty good."

"Pretty good? That was fabulous. Very important for you. One down, several more to go. Alan's house is next. Let's hope we do as well there."

"Dan Murphy's quite a guy. Doesn't waste a minute, does he?"

"Yep, I've worked for him for quite awhile. He sure knows what he's doing, and, of course, I help just a little bit."

"No, Bernie, you were great."

"Thanks, I was waiting for that."

We drove up Alan's imposing driveway past the tall hedges. This was first time I entered his estate that way since the night of the party and it gave me chills to be reminded of how happy Melody and I were as we drove up in that cab, so happy to be back with each other again. I felt much older now. As a matter of fact I felt like an old man compared to those carefree moments just a few days ago.

"Let me do all the talking. I'll handle this."

"It's all yours, Bernie."

Sydney the butler came to the door after Bernie banged the big gong. I never noticed Alan had a Chinese gong.

"What can I do for you?" What are you doing here?"

Sydney was surprised to see me there. He probably thought I was still safely tucked away in some prison cell.

"I can't talk to you. Mr. Prescott is not here."

"Oh, I didn't come to talk to you Boris, but I got a court order here that says we can come into this house and take a look around."

"My name is not Boris, it's Sydney. Let me see that paper."

"Bernie waved the paper in front of him, "It's a court order, signed by the District Attorney."

"How do I know it's real, authentic?"

"Why don't you call the D.A.'s office."

"O.K., come on in, but don't touch anything and I'll have to accompany you."

"Accompany all you want. Let's start with the room downstairs."

I led Bernie, followed by the bozo Sydney, a big tall hulking man. We went downstairs, past the Rothko paintings, past the screening room. Bernie tried the handle to the now "storage" room. The door was locked.

"O.K. I need you to unlock this door."

"I can't. I don't have the key."

"Well I guess I'll just have to break it down."

"You don't have the right to do that." Sydney raised his voice and, at over six foot tall, he towered over Bernie in a menacing way.

"This paper says I do." Bernie waved the paper.

Sydney blocked the door, "Well I say you don't."

"Wait right here while I make a call."

Bernie dialed a number. "Hey Sam, I'm at Alan Prescott's house. Can you send your finest over. We have a problem searching the premises, and we can't get into one of the rooms. Great. Send him right over."

"An officer will be here in about three minutes. Mind if we wait here. We want to make sure the room's not tampered with before we get in, that is any more tampered with than it already was."

Bernie was pretty comical all right. He just stood there calmly and lit up one of his foul smelling stogies, and then put the butt out right on Alan's floor, all the while humming the tune to the Dragnet T.V. show. Sydney did not look amused.

A few minutes later, the door bell rang.

"Don't touch anything 'till I get back. Sydney hurried upstairs.

A few minutes later a large burly looking guy in plain clothes came clomping down the stairs.

"Hey Bernie, you up to no good?"

"That's right, Rob. Think you can help me with this door without damaging it too much? Don't want to damage anything here," Bernie shot a dirty look at Sydney.

"No problem." Rob took out some tools, fiddled around a few minutes with the lock, and then stepped back as he swung the door open. "After you."

The room still had all the furniture in it, covered over just like the last time I was there.

"Here Bernie, you need to look over here." I pointed to where the chains had been attached, but now they were covered by an ornate mirror and two big landscape paintings in gilded frames.

"Hey Rob, give me a hand with these." The two of them removed the mirror and the paintings and leant them up against the wall.

"Well, well, well, look what we have here." There were six patches of plaster over where the chains had been attached, just like I said, for the three sets of chains. Bernie ran his finger over one of them. "Hey, this plaster's still damp." Then he took several photos.

"Hey Rob, can you help me push some of this furniture out of the way, against the walls."

Then Bernie got on his hands and knees and started crawling around on the floor with a magnifying glass. He stopped at one spot about in the middle of the floor.

"I think I'll take an itsy bitsy sample right here."

He took a tweezer out of a case and lifted something from between the floor boards, something so small nobody had apparently seen it. He placed the sample in a tube and put a cap on it.

"We'll see what we can see when this baby is put under a microscope and tested by the lab."

Bernie continued to hunt around on the floor, until his knee brushed against something under a small rug.

"Well, well, well, what do we got here?" he said as he stood up and kicked the rug back. It revealed the trap door. Bernie opened the trap door and saw the safe, which was locked.

"Sydney, would you like to open that."

Sydney wouldn't move a muscle and looked so angry like he about to burst a blood vessel.

"I know, you don't have the key, right? Sydney just nodded.

"Officer Rob, we're going to need your services again."

"No problem."

In about ten seconds, Rob opened the safe. Bernie took out three reels of 16 mm film. "I'm going to confiscate these in case there is evidence and people to question in any of these films."

"You can't take those. They belong to Mr. Prescott." He tried to block Bernie.

Bernie waved the paper again in front Sydney, "Get out of the way or you'll be done with obstructing justice."

Sydney reluctantly moved back. I guess there was only so far he was willing to go for Alan. Bernie put the three reels into his briefcase.

"How about that rug Michael? Do you see it anywhere?"

"No, I don't think so. They must have gotten rid of it."

"O.K. Let's go. I think I have what I need."

We walked outside to Bernie's car, the three of us.

"Thanks Rob for helping out." Bernie handed Rob a wad of cash. "At least I found something. That sample looks like a speck of dried blood to me."

"Great Bernie. At least we're finally making some progress." I said as I slipped into the passenger seat of Bernie's beat up LeBaron.

"I'll drop you off. Then I'm going straight to the lab. I'll let you know as soon as we get the results."

"Great."

I noticed as Rob pulled out that he wasn't in a police car. Bernie then drove us down the long winding driveway.

"Is Rob really a police officer?"

"Well, sort of, he's a security guard at Walton's. That's like a deputized police officer."

"Bernie! So will the search hold up?"

"You let me worry about that."

"O.K."

"Then I'll get that interview with Alan's neighbor transcribed, come back here and get him to sign it," Bernie said puffing on his stogie.

Just as we were about to enter the road, Alan pulled up in his Bugatti replicar and blocked Bernie's car.

"What the hell are you doing here! Michael, I thought you were ... "

"In prison. Is that what you were going to say. No, I'm out on bail, as you can see, thanks to Sybil."

"That ungrateful wretch. You better get off my property right now. What are you doing here?"

"We were here on official business. I have the paper to show it."

When Bernie held the paper out, Alan grabbed it, as their windows were that close.

"Wait a minute. Let me see that. Why this is bullshit. This isn't an official document. It says this is a warranty for one year for parts and labor for a chemical toilet for a Bowrider."

"Let me see that." Bernie grabbed it back. "Oh, I guess you're right. It must have gotten mixed up on my desk. It's very messy."

"I'll have your for this. Did Sydney let you into the house?"

"Yes he did. So you see, officially, we were invitees, guests, and were there quite legally."

"Who's that guy who just drove out of here?"

"Oh him, he was a guest too, let in by Sydney, your butler."

"Get the hell off my property." Alan was beside himself, about to blow a gasket.

"Just a minute." Bernie jumped out of his car and walked to the front of the Bugatti.

"This is strange." Bernie quickly snapped a few photos of the front of Alan's car.

"What the hell are you doing now. I told you to get off my property!"

Bernie jumped back in the driver's seat saying, "I didn't know they put dabs of blue paint on the front of forest green Bugattis."

Bernie backed up and soon we were breezing back to Sybil's. I felt about one ton lighter. Everything felt better, and I could breathe a bit easier now.

"Bernie, you were great. I really thought you had a court order to search Alan's house."

"No, but being a good bull shitter really helps in this business. I think Dan will like what we're coming up with so far."

"Why didn't the police get any of this?"

"'Cause it didn't help their case."

"Aren't I supposed to be innocent until proven guilty."

"That's exactly what they were trying to prove, that you're guilty. Out here in the field, they only find what they want to find, and they only know what they want to believe. That's the way it works."

"Thanks, Bernie."

"Let's not get our hopes up yet, but it's a good start."

Bernie dropped me off at Sybil's glass masterpiece of a house. I ran straight upstairs when I heard her talking. She was in her bedroom just hanging up the phone. I grabbed her, pushed her over onto her bed, and pulled off her clothes as she tore at mine. Then we made love for hours and hours, mad passionate love, over and over again. We just couldn't get enough of each other. I was becoming addicted to her and I had to have her all the time.

CHAPTER 17 - Wednesday, August 6, East Hampton

A few hours later, Dan Murphy phoned to say that the speck Bernie got off the floor was blood and they were running an analysis of it to see if it matched Eric's. But the problem was that was the room Alan and his confreres said I fought with Eric, and that's why his blood was there. To make matters worse, when the police came back to Alan's house, they found the smashed up Ray Bans in the same room. Naturally, the sunglasses had both mine and Eric's fingerprints all over them. Alan was a tough adversary and he was still up and fighting in round two.

The blue paint on the front of Alan's Bugatti was the exact type the factory used on the 1989 Buick, the butler's car. At least that was the color it was before it was burnt black. But Alan said he ran into the back of the Sydney's car in the driveway one night when the house lights hadn't been turned on. He had an answer for everything.

Dan Murphy wasn't satisfied with the first lab test of the speck of blood Bernie found, so he wanted a more expensive test with the latest technology run on it. But to Sybil, money was no object in trying to protect me, so he got her permission and went ahead with it. When the results came back from the independent lab, they found something very interesting. They found submicroscopic particles of human tissue, from a colon, mixed in with the blood. It began to look like Alan should have hired a better cleaning service. I thought this was the one break Dan was looking for.

Well, Dan was starting to prove why he drove a Rolls Royce and had a nice size yacht moored at the Southampton Yacht Club. The man was smart, damn smart, and he didn't mind hiring someone a little bent, like Bernie, as long he got the job done. Bernie apparently knew how to stay just this side of the law, but just barely.

The testimony from the neighbor confirmed what I had said about how and when I left Alan's that night, through the back gate. Then there was Maria, the maid's statement, signed and sworn that she saw me back at Sybil's house at 3:00 A.M. that Saturday night, the night of the murder. And most important, there was that tiny blood sample, of Eric's blood. Poor Eric. Things were certainly starting to look up for my side of the story.

Then, that evening, Dan Murphy pulled up in Sybil's driveway in his light blue Rolls Royce Corniche convertible, and unbelievable as it was after all that, he started talking about a plea deal. I just about blew my top, but somehow managed to barely contain myself.

He wanted me to make a plea deal, but to a lesser charge.

"Are you kidding! After all this? You want me to make a plea bargain?" I could hardly believe it.

"Look kid, I'm going to be perfectly honest with you..."

"What, you're going to hang me out to dry, just like the public defender. I don't believe it!" Maybe Sybil didn't want to spend all that money for a trial and Dan Murphy was very expensive, plus all the experts and whatever.

"Sure, I'd like to go for a trial, and get myself lots of publicity on a sensational case like this, double murder. It always gets my firm new clients. But in your case, it's not such a good idea."

"Why not? I thought we were doing great, with all this new evidence."

"Yeah, great enough to go the D.A. and try to get you a better deal, much better than you would have gotten before. Because, see, I'm only starting to damage his case a little, but not totally. So now he has to think, what are the chances of the prosecutor winning in court. Well, sure, his chances have gone down a little, but not totally. So that puts us in a better position to get a better deal."

"Better than the twenty years that dick head was going to get me?"

"No comparison. But remember, there's one charge that going to stick no matter what."

"And what's that."

"Accessory. Accessory to murder."

"Even though I was tied up when it happened. And that I wasn't there when they murdered poor Melody?"

"Yes. You failed to report it immediately after you returned to Sybil's house. You might have been able to save Melody's life. The fact that she was being held there against her will and was a witness to Eric's murder, it placed her in imminent danger."

"So you're saying there's no getting out of that charge, right?"

"They can still say you caused Eric's fatal injury with the knife they found with your fingerprints on it, in spite of the lab evidence."

"Great. Looks like I'm right back where I started from. Am I still facing a long jail term?"

"I don't think so, but I'll see what I can do. I'm not promising a miracle. You're going to get some time, but I need your permission to start the process. Then we'll see what we got."

"You're starting to sound just like Kapp."

"Michael, it's the only way, believe me. For your benefit, it's what I'm recommending."

"What about Syil? What does she say?"

"She agrees you should go along with what I'm recommending. I guess she has more confidence in me than you do."

"O.K., I guess. Find out what he's offering this time. And it better be good, much, much better. I'm not going to rot in some prison cell for years. That's definitely out, way out."

"That a boy and it'll save Sybil a lot of money too, not going through a long, drawn out trial where your chances of winning are right now about fifty-fifty."

"So that's it. Is that why you won't go to trial, the cost?"

"No, that's not it at all. In my assessment, your chances of winning are about only fifty-fifty, plus the capricious element of any jury trial. No, that's not it. Now, don't go getting paranoid on me. After all she's done for you. I just don't like the risk of this trial, that's all. It doesn't feel right. There's something about it I don't like."

"So it's not Sybil, about going through with the trial?

I thought we were going to win."

"Before I spoke to you, I talked to Sybil on the phone, and she wanted to go through with the trial, but I talked her out of it. At first she insisted on it. She said she didn't care how much it cost, but I was the one who talked her out of it. And to think how much of that fee just got flushed down the toilet. I could have built my family a nice villa in the South of France."

"You talked her out of it?"

"Yes, I'm afraid so. I think I'm getting too altruistic. It really is in your best interest. Yes, it's definitely the right thing to do. Take my word for it. Remember, I told you I like to win, even more than I like making money."

"Well, that certainly separates you from most lawyers."

"I guess so."

"Remember what Mao did after the Revolution?"

"What was that?"

"They rounded up all the lawyers in each precinct, and had them all shot by firing squads."

"Remember Michael, I still have to represent you."

"Mao called them parasites, that's it, parasites, because they feed off society without ever producing anything."

"Michael now, I better get out of here before I decide to join the prosecution."

"You wouldn't do that."

"We're not all bad, you know. I'll call you as soon as I've met with the D.A."

"When's that. Your next golfing date?"

"No, I'm meeting him at his office. I told him I'd see him after speaking with you. I'll call you later."

After Dan Murphy drove off in his Rolls, I didn't feel too good. Plea bargain, again, after all that. Facing time, locked up. I didn't know if I could handle it again. And after all the build up I got from Bernie's investigation. Sybil wasn't too happy with the thought of me locked up again, even for a short time.

Sybil came out of the house asking, "So how did it go?"

"Not well."

"I thought I'd better just let you two talk it out by yourselves. After all, it's your life and it should be your decision. What did you decide?"

"I told him to find out about the plea deal, on the reduced charge of accessory. To see what he could get. Sometimes life isn't fair, but I guess you have to take the bad with the good."

"Speaking of bad, what's Alan doing here?"

Alan came roaring up Sybil's driveway in his Bugatti. He was by himself. He had a long scarf around his neck, just like some old time movie tycoon.

"What the hell are you doing here Alan? You're not welcome here ever again." Sybil was not happy to see him.

"I hope you fry in hell, and the way it's going you just might end up doing that," I added.

"I just came to say I'm sorry Sybil, I'm sorry about everything's that happened. I didn't want to pull the plug on your picture, but you didn't give me much choice. Besides you were over budget and behind schedule, with all that location shooting. The studio was going to do it anyways."

"You had choices, Alan, and you took them. I never want to see you again."

"You shouldn't have sided against me, your best friend, your biggest supporter. And it was your fault, anyways."

"What the hell are you talking about!" Sybil shouted.

"How dare you come here and blame her, you son of a bitch. You better get out of here right now, or I might kill you with my bare hands, but scum like you aren't worth killing. It'll only get more time, thanks to you, you slimy bastard."

Michael tried to reach for Alan, but Sybil tried to hold him back.

"Hey," Alan started backing up and turned his car around.

"I only came here to try to make a truce with you. I just came up here to tell you things didn't happen the way I intended."

"No, they certainly didn't, not after I hired Dan Murphy."

"Yes, it's starting to look like they're going to try to twist things around against me. And the scandal is mounting in the tabloids. It's not looking too good for me. The studio chief wants me out in L.A. for a meeting right away, and I'm not looking forward to that at all. I'm really sorry, Sybil, sorry about everything that's happened. Adieu, mes amis, je vais a la gloire."

I broke loose from Sybil's tight grip and lunged towards Alan just before he started down the driveway. I grabbed him around his neck. I wanted to strangle him for all he's done, all the pain he caused, but he roared off so fast trying to get away from me that his car spun out of control and crashed into a huge tree at the bottom of the driveway. It didn't look like Alan was moving. The wheels were still spinning with the car turned on its side.

Sybil and I ran down to Alan's car. The long scarf had caught in the wire wheels of his Bugatti and saved me the trouble of strangling him.

As I looked at the crumpled up front end of the Bugatti, I said, "What a waste of a car."

"Michael, I think he's dead."

"You're damn right he's dead. His fucking neck is broken."

"Michael, this is no time to be joking. I've got to call the police."

"Let me put it this way. I wasn't too fond of Alan and I'm not at all sorry to see him gone, before he could hurt any more people."

"Funny, Isadora Duncan, the famous American dancer, died the same way, and in a Bugatti too, only a real one."

"Quite a coincidence."

"She said the same words as Alan did as he drove off."

"What do those words mean?"

"It's French for 'Goodbye my friends, I am going to my glory."

"Do you think he meant to kill himself?"

"No, Alan loved himself too much for that. He just liked to make others suffer. Everything had to be high drama for him."

"Do you think they would have gotten him through the court system?"

"No, he was too rich and powerful. He had everyone in his pocket. Political contributions and the like all the way up the line."

"Well, it looks like Eric got his revenge anyways."

"You better call Dan Murphy and the police. Don't wait another minute Sybil, or they might call you an accessory."

"The only accessory I'm going to be is wrapped around you all night long."

"Now that's an accessory I could go for, all night long."

Maria came running down the driveway, "What happened, Madame, what has happened?"

"Maria, call the police right away. Tell them there's been an accident, a terrible accident, but tell them not to bother about rushing an ambulance over. It's too late for that."

"What, Madame!"

"Yes, a terrible accident. We weren't here."

"Yes, Madame."

"And we're not here now. In fact, we're leaving right now for the Yacht Club. I need a strong Long Island ice tea after that."

"Oh yes, Madame.' Maria took in the gory sight below."

As they got into Sybil's jeep, Michael asked, "Was that really the way Isadora Duncan died?"

As Sybil inched her way carefully down the winding driveway past Alan's car, she answered, "Well, sort of. She was in the passenger seat with a handsome young Italian mechanic who was driving her home in her Bugatti. They took off down the road after a party. She was forty-nine at the time and had been a famous dancer. What she really meant was she was going to make glorious love with the mechanic, and in that sense she was going to her glory, that kind of ecstatic glory from love making.

Instead, a few yards down the road, right in front of all the guests who were on the terrace at the party, her shawl got caught in one of the wire wheels of her Bugatti and broke her neck. She died immediately, just like Alan."

"That's pretty scary, when you come to think of it."

"Yes, fate can be pretty scary, sometimes. You just never know what's going to happen next. That's why we better grab it all while we can."

Instead of going to the Yacht Club for that Long Island ice tea, Sybil drove us to a small quaint inn just outside of town. We went straight to a room with chintz rose patterned curtains and a matching quilt bedspread. We tore off each other's clothes, and we made torrid love for the rest of the afternoon, over and over again. We were insatiable for each other's bodies.

The police arrived and made their report as they questioned Maria. An ambulance took Alan's lifeless body, covered with the proverbial white sheet, on a stretcher out to the morgue.

Later we returned to Sybil's house and soon all was quiet again. A cool breeze blew in through an open window, and it seemed to fan our insatiable desire for each other, as once again our bodies entwined themselves and our lips joined together. We became like some sort of primordial creature, self-fornicating in the sea before it separated itself into its male and female parts and became two separate entities, forever at odds with its other part, a friction that seemed never to end on down through the ages.

POSTSCRIPT - Autumn

Well, Dan Murphy, Attorney Dan Murphy, went and negotiated a plea deal the very next day. It seems he told the prosecutor that he would hand him a very wealthy client of his, a big drug dealer that they were about to try in court the very next week, if he would let me off as light as possible. When I asked him why he decided to hand over that wealthy client of his, he said it was because he didn't want to see a nice young guy like me go away behind bars for a very long time, when very likely I was innocent. I didn't like the way he said, "very likely." The fact that Sybil offered him a speaking part in her next film as an attorney, he said, had absolutely nothing to do with it. Right. He convinced the prosecutor the conviction of a big drug dealer would look better on his record, in spite of the sensationalism surrounding my trial. He told him that he'd have a better chance of winning the election than with the possible conviction of a lowly nobody like me. I wasn't too flattered by his description, but with Alan dead, the wind kind of went out of the prosecutor's sails anyways. And as it turned out, Alan was a major contributor to the prosecutor's campaign. He sure knew how to play his cards right. As they say, the spigot from Alan got turned off.

I was certain I was going to get some lengthy prison time on this plea bargaining thing. When I went in front of the judge, I couldn't believe it when I heard myself say "Guilty," to the charge of Accessory to Murder." I got five years, suspended sentence and two years of probation. Dan had convinced the prosecutor to drop the murder and rape charges. There was one hitch, though. I had to do community service, lots of community service, 500 hours worth. And I had to do it on Long Island. I didn't care. I really didn't want to go back to Manhattan anyways. I'd had my fill of that rat's nest.

Well, the police never even looked for Ernest. They all thought I had entirely made him up, as some sort of cover. But in the end, they blamed it all on Alan, the dead man. It's easier and neater than way. For dead men can't talk. And he really was responsible for it anyways. So Alan's dirty little secret was out and it certainly didn't leave him a very nice obituary. The tabloid headlines that week screamed out, "FILM MOGUL COMMITS SUICIDE AS HE WAS ABOUT TO BE CHARGED WITH A GRISLY SEX-SLAY MURDER."

That's the tabloids for you. You know they always twist everything around, but they know how to word it just right so they don't get sued, at least most of the time. Melody's car wreck was ruled a homicide, not an accident.

Alan's wife Ingrid had a nervous breakdown and entered an alcohol and drug abuse program at the Betty Ford Clinic. The last we heard of her, she was seeing some tall blond younger guy who was there at the Clinic for the same problems. Annize got so upset about Sybil's film getting shut down, she hired a top notch entertainment lawyer and sued the studio. The studio was so upset she was suing them for breach of contract that the studio chief vowed she would never work in Hollywood again. So she sold her wonderful triplex loft in Manhattan and moved out to Malibu with Don. I later found out that Ernest didn't run for Governor of California, but I was close. It turned out he was a Senator from California. Imagine that, and he's still there in Congress, influencing important decisions with his votes.

Sybil was as wonderful as ever and our relationship just grew stronger with each passing day. It was the beginning of September now, and she had to go back to Manhattan to start her new picture, a murder mystery. It had the working title, "The Endless Summer." She had gotten an independent studio to back it. She was letting me stay at the beach house in East Hampton and she was going to come out every weekend. I wasn't going to be there much anyways, with 500 hours of community service to do. Good thing she left me the keys to her Jeep, to use whenever

I wanted.

It was autumn now, and the weather was cooling down. Most of the tourists and summer residents had left the Hamptons and traffic had become a lot more tolerable. Even the seagulls seemed happier that the crush of humanity had left and crawled its way back to Manhattan.

It seems when the heat of summer starts to let up, we start to act more sensibly, more with our heads. When the first autumn leaves start to fall, our primal urges begin to get more under control. I was glad the dog days of summer were gone, those final hot days that make us feel stuck in our distress and the hopelessness of the human condition. When our most animal instincts act up and tempers flare, it's when wars start and all kinds of human folly and foul behavior take place.

I did make one trip off the island that I didn't tell anyone about. I went to see Melody's parents in Queens. I felt I owed it to them, to help them put closure to the terrible loss of their daughter. They were expecting me after I called them the day before and explained I had been a friend of their daughter at the acting school. I had grown a moustache and told them my name was John Smith. There was no sense in upsetting them any further. They were very nice people and they treated me like a son. They were like the parents I never had. They put out a nice lunch in their brownstone and we spent the whole time talking about Melody and how wonderful and talented she was. Then we drove out together to Melody's gravesite and I laid down a huge array of the flowers I bought. I hate to admit it, but I couldn't hold back the tears that trickled down my face. My back was to them, so I hope they didn't see my silent crying. I was a man and men weren't supposed to cry. But the sight of the white gladiolas mixed with the long stem red roses, the lilies, the purple hyacinths and the delicate sprays of white baby's breath against the cold gray headstone just got to me and it choked me up. Then I looked down the long line of trees and I swear I saw her walking towards me, floating, smiling her beautiful smile. But she just kept walking past me, smiling off into the distance in her white tulle dress, the one she wore that night.

When I returned to Sybil's house later that afternoon, Sybil had come in from Manhattan to spend the weekend with me. She asked where I had been and I didn't want to lie to her anymore, but I told her I had just done some community service. She looked at me suspiciously since I did have on a grey suit. I said I had changed before coming home so I would look nice for her.

Sybil offered to send me back to The Strasberg Institute when the community service was over, but I couldn't. I just couldn't handle ever being back there because all it would do was remind me of Melody. You see, I never got over that and I never will. Things like that affect you for the rest of your life. They never really leave your mind, no matter what you're doing or who you're doing it with.

But I have to admit, for the first time I felt like I didn't need to keep moving, looking around the corner for the next thrill. Maybe I was getting older at twenty-five. I'd been through a lot that summer, and it felt good to be in one place with one person.

At this time, anyway, I had no desire to go out to Hollywood to seek fame and fortune. I thought, at least for now, I had it all right here, a great lover who really seemed to care about me and came through in my darkest hour, no matter what the cost to her was, and it was a great cost. Bonded me out by risking her house, and that caused the shut down of her picture by Alan. Maybe it was going to be shut down anyways, I didn't want to take responsibility for that. Alan had said the completion bond people were about to take it over anyways, for being over budget and behind schedule.

Then there was the fantastic beach right outside to use any time I wanted, at least when I wasn't picking up liter on the side of the roads and other nasty jobs. And I had the use of the red Jeep to use any time I wanted.

But the bottom line was, I had gotten a lot more serious. For some of the community service, I chose to work at the local prison, the one I had been incarcerated at, Riverhead Correctional

Facility. It was about half an hour and three worlds away from East Hampton. I did the community service in the theatre workshop, of all things. I was teaching acting and preparing to put on a play with the inmates as the actors and as the scenery designers and stage hands. It was better than picking up cigarette butts in the park.

The funny thing is one of my students turned out to be Herman, who had helped me when a man can threaten his own existence and lose faith in everything, and think he has no future. Herman was great. I owed him a lot, he probably saved my life. He had such a wonderful voice, I thought maybe he could be the next Morgan Freeman. He definitely had real potential.
The play I had them preparing to present at the prison was Hamlet. Herman was magnificent as Hamlet, saying, "Aye, there's the rub, for in that sleep of death, what dreams may come when we have shuffled off this mortal coil must give us pause. There's the respect that makes calamity of so long a life for who

would bear the whips and scorns of time, the oppressors' wrong, the proud man's contumely, the pangs of despised love, the law's delays, the insolence of office and spurns that patient merit of the unworthy takes when he himself his quietus make with a bare bodkin." A bodlin is a dagger.

Yes, Herman was great as Hamlet. He really seemed to really feel those lines. The next black Lawrence Olivier, I thought. But after seeing the blank looks on the faces of the inmates after listening to this famous speech in Old English written by Shakespeare, I decided to rework the play in a version that would be more suited to its current audience.

Herman stood up and began in his wonderful voice with the new version of those same lines, "Hey man, there's the thing, for in the sleep of death, what dreams you have when you drop dead from this life forever, you might not like them. Yeah, that's why we put up with all this crap and try to live a nice long life, and bear the whips and scorns of time, put up with the foot of the oppressors, the bullshit from your bosses, the heartbreak of spurned love, the long delays of the law courts, the cheating and lying of the politicians. And sometimes you're so fed up, you think of taking a knife and doing yourself in. But who would put up with all this bullshit and sweat long hours all your life long, but for the fear of what comes after death, that undiscovered country from where no traveler returns. Yeah, it makes us put up with all the crap that's flung at us, than to go to something maybe more terrible that we know nothing about. Yes, the fear of death and what may come after, or nothing at all, surely makes cowards of us all."

When he was done this time, the inmates, my cast and crew, stood up and broke into wild cheers and stamped their feet. Herman was magnificent. Now we were ready to prepare the rest of the play to put on in front of the whole prison, the guards and even the warden and his wife, except of course those in solitary confinement or those too violent to attend the performance.

Herman never let me forget that I didn't get him that carton of Camels, the one I promised him, the day I was released on the bond Sybil put up for me. So every time I came, I brought him that promised carton. Since Herman was due to be released on parole in just three months, I thought I could guide him to try out for an off-Broadway play, or even Broadway. After all, I did owe him my life. He had stopped me from hanging myself in the middle of the night on a bed sheet when I thought I was facing twenty years of hell. Of course that was before Sybil finally came through with Dan Murphy, and before Bernie's investigative talents. And don't forget, Dan Murphy's skills with getting me that suspended sentence.

I didn't particularly like the drive back alone at dusk to the beach house, past the cornfields, the empty dunes, the tall pampas grass and field after field of pumpkins, because, well, it gave me too much time to think, and I wasn't ready for that. I was always relieved to be pulling up to that driveway.

When I was back at the house, the first thing I always did was run down to the beach and just stand there for a moment watching the tides go in and out, and listen to the ear piercing shrieks of the sea gulls as they swooped down to the sand.

I would just stand there with the cold autumn wind whipping at my back and watch those sea gulls darting down to the churning ocean, then picking up seaweed, twigs and all sort of debris from the beach. Maybe they were building a nest.

As I stood there, I decided I never wanted to go back to Manhattan. I just wanted to stay out here and wait for the weekends when Sybil would be pulling up in her black limo, and wait for the hours of pleasure we would enjoy in each other's arms. I liked the fresh smell of the air blowing in off the ocean, and I was determined to turn my life around. I promised myself that I would be absolutely faithful to her, for I realized she was all I ever really needed. In fact, I still wear her ring, the one with her initial "S" embossed in gold, and it was never going to come off. It couldn't. The ends of the ring that pierced through my nipple had been soldered together. And I had no desire to have it removed. I was hers, forever.

POST- POSTSCRIPT - Autumn, East Hampton

One Friday when Michael was waiting for Sybil to return from New York for their long weekend together, he ran short of cash. He needed to buy a pack of cigarettes, having taken up the habit when he was in prison. He looked everywhere for change, even in the sofas downstairs. He knew Sybil wouldn't be back for hours, especially with the Friday evening traffic.

Finally, desperate, he went to Sybil's desk in her bedroom and broke open the lock. Inside the top drawer, he found a book. It was her diary. He knew he shouldn't, but he couldn't resist. He opened the book and started reading. He couldn't believe what was written there in Sybil's own handwriting. He was right. He should have never opened that diary. Sybil knew about the whole thing, that Saturday night after all. He could hardly believe what he was reading that was written there on those pages.

"Alan called me right after Michael and that girl arrived at his party. He told me they were there, and they seemed too cozy, kissing and making out just beyond the terrace area around the pool. He said that Michael was on the loose with that pretty young thing, and that they were still at his house. He asked me what he should do.

I told him to get rid of her and to send Michael back to my house with his driver. Alan agreed to get rid of her but only if he could have his fun first. I foolishly agreed, but I told him to get him away from the girl and make sure she never shows up out here again.'

When I told Alan to get rid of her, I didn't know he was going to kill her. All I meant was to put her on the train, to get her out of East Hampton, get her away from Michael. And somehow scare her so much that she would never want to come back. I didn't know he was going to kill her.

Now I have no choice. He's going to frame Michael for the murder. I'm going to have to help him go up against Alan, my best friend and my biggest supporter. In a way, it was my fault. I should have never told him to get rid of her. But I guess he took it the wrong way."

Michael felt dizzy and had to sit down. He had to think of what he would say to Sybil when she returned later than night. Maybe it would be best, he thought, if he said nothing. Really, it was for the best. The past couldn't be undone. And in spite of what she said, or what she might have done, he was still hers and there was no one else he wanted to be with, and nowhere else he wanted to be, but holding her close to him. He looked forward to the hours of lovemaking, to the passion of hours of holding her close to him. Yes, he thought, he belonged to her, and he wanted to be hers, forever.

&&&&&&&&&&&&&&&&&&&&&&&&&